BADFISH

BADFISH

▲ ▲ ▲

Sue Rovens

ISBN: 1515110303
ISBN 13: 9781515110309

Acknowledgements

▲ ▲ ▲

VERY SPECIAL HEARTFELT THANKS TO all of the people listed on this page.

Without their generosity through Kickstarter, this book would not have been possible:

Carol and Dr. Stephen Cann
David Cann
James Semmelroth Darnell
Charlie "The Quaker" Edwards
Mary Lynn Edwards
Howard Francis
Carolyn Gerberding
VyAnn Grant
Carol J. Hartzell
Janet Kuebli
Katherine Nichols
Carolyn Shaffer
Karen Shaw
Grant Young
Marcy Young

and extra special thanks to:
Dr. Stephen Cann - Props Master for the Kickstarter Video
Charlie "The Quaker" Edwards – Voice Over for the Kickstarter Video

Table of Contents

For Clarence
Forever and then some
-Lillian

CHAPTER 1

BICKLEY

▲ ▲ ▲

DONALD BICKLEY HAD A REPUTATION of being a mean son-of-a-bitch just like his dad, Roger. When Donald and his brothers were growing up on the farm, Roger liked to sneak up from behind and kick them right smack between their legs. He'd let out a hardy belly laugh as he watched the young Bickleys fall to their knees and grab their groins in agony. When he was feeling particularly devilish, he would stand next to the electric fence that kept the cows in and call Donald over to help him with something. When his youngest son would run over to see what was needed, Roger would simultaneously grab the fence and Donald at the same time. That little trick sent the two older brothers into fits of laughter while Roger just smirked. Then he would scold Donald, telling him not to be so damn gullible and womanlike.

Roger Bickley's family owned the farm free and clear since before the start of World War I. They raised cattle, corn, and chickens before Donald and his brothers came along. By the time Roger's wife was pregnant for the third time, farm life had become too daunting for her. The stress of raising two wild boys while trying to survive an abusive marriage on top of everything else led to her untimely demise. Seven months later, Roger Bickley's wife passed on in childbirth, a little factoid that Donald's dad never seemed to let him forget, as if it were *his* fault.

As early as Donald could remember, the farm always came first, a strong fear of God came second, and if there was enough time in the day, family came a distant third. Keeping food on the table and a roof over head were the primary reasons to get up in the morning and get your ass out into the fields. Fortunately for Donald, being the youngest Bickley also meant having the easiest work load.

He was put in charge of the chickens, which meant early mornings of gathering eggs, spreading feed, and general cleaning. Since his dad and brothers were usually busy with more labor-intensive farm work, he could sneak away and spend hours among the rows of laying hens, confiding in them his thoughts, his fears and his darkest secrets. As the years passed, Donald had plenty of dark secrets that burdened him.

Eventually, his brothers got married and bought farms of their own, leaving only Donald and his dad to live in the main house. Two men alone couldn't run the large working farm, so Roger hired some local hands to help with the demanding fieldwork. Donald continued to look after the chickens and also took over the household duties like cooking, cleaning, and laundry. It wasn't ideal, but there was always food on the table and clean beds to sleep in at the end of the day.

Fortunately for Donald, there was always a great deal of work to do. Most days, he could find enough chores to keep busy until

Roger went up to bed. But on occasion, he would find himself sitting across from his father at the dining room table. Those evenings filled him with dread; swimming in a pool of awkwardness and loathing that made him wish he had the guts to move out. On those particular evenings after supper was served, eaten, and put away, Roger would pull at his earlobe and Donald returned the gesture with the smallest of head nods.

It was during those very specific moments that his stomach would turn. His gut filled with acid that crept up into his throat and burned every inch of his intestinal lining. He hated that gesture. He hated the meaning behind it. He hated his father and his brothers every time they did it. But instead of fighting or cussing or dismissing it, Donald would lower his head and solemnly climb the two flights of stairs in the center of the old farm house. He would enter the small bedroom and open the closet door where his eyes would rest on the yellow flowered dress that had been his mother's favorite church outfit. He would take it off the hanger, throw it on the bed, and remove his overalls and plaid shirt.

He would hear Roger's labored breathing as his father ascended the wooden staircase, pausing for a moment on the second floor landing. As tough as Roger was, the years had started to take a toll on him by this point. Hard manual labor helped keep him in shape, but the body can only stand so much for so long. He had started to feel every pain and twinge these days when he went from the corn crib to the shed. Normal routines were taking a little longer with each passing season. But he would be damned to hell before he buckled under and saw Doc

Norton for little aches and pains. He just told himself that he wasn't working hard enough, that he was getting lazy. 'Hard work is a cure-all for anything,' Roger's father used to say. And if it was good enough for *his* dad, it was good enough for him and his sons.

Donald would squeeze himself into the dress and sit on the bed facing away from the door. Repulsion would flood his body as he listened for the familiar creak of the wooden floor and the heavy foot falls that echoed off the walls. Without looking, he knew the exact sequence of events that were taking place right behind his back. The flickering of the light switch, the removal of Roger's clothes, the placement of his shirt and pants on the chair next to the dresser. The next few minutes were the worst; worse than the sex act itself.

Roger would stand behind him and rub his shoulders, easing his way down Donald's arms to his thighs and finally to his crotch. Physiologically, Donald couldn't help but become hard from the stroking and rubbing, even though it disgusted him to his core. Roger would bend down and kiss his neck while unbuttoning the front of the dress until he could run his hands over Donald's naked flesh. Without a word, Donald would turn and lie on his stomach while Roger lifted the long yellow skirt up far enough to expose his buttocks. A quick handful of lube from the square green container of Bag Balm, which was conveniently placed on the night stand next to the bed, made Roger's entry into the tormented chasm of Donald's impenetrable anus a little less problematic.

By this time, Donald's thoughts were far away. After years of being the surrogate female for his father and brothers, he was able to imagine himself somewhere, *anywhere* other than where he actually was at that moment. While it had crossed his mind over the years to leave the family farm, there had always been an impending sense of loyalty and responsibility that was too overwhelming to fight against. That, and the fact that he could never leave his chickens.

When Roger finally passed away in the 1970s, Donald sold the farm and made enough money to get his own house, open the only strip joint in Badfish, and have a very sizable nest egg in the bank. By severing all contact with his brothers, Donald Bickley was confident that no one ever knew, save some chickens, what *really* took place during those years in the white farm house on Springfield Lane, ten miles outside of Badfish.

CHAPTER 2

THE FINCHON MOTEL

▲ ▲ ▲

THE FINCHON MOTEL HAD PERCHED over the small town of Badfish for the past fifty years. During that time, the small community idly watched the rise and the subsequent fall of this business as it morphed from being the proverbial swinging hot spot in the 1960s, to a popular haunt for up and coming trendsetters of the 70s and 80s, to what it eventually became - an eyesore that housed mostly unwashed transients and drug-addled dope fiends.

The Badfish County Visitor's Bureau and the town's own residents duly praised the Finchon during its early years. Tourists who inquired about local lodging were encouraged to stay there. It was a perfect complement to the boutiques and novelty stores that dotted the small downtown area. But now, not even Donald Bickley would set foot in the place.

Eight years ago, after the previous owner had passed away from losing a bout with cancer, the Finchon went on the market. The motel had begun to suffer from neglect a few years prior to the man's demise. Minor problems turned into major issues, and by the time hospice was called, the place was in serious need of renovations and repairs.

Karl Demetris, a local man, bought the motel and promised the town's board that their high expectations for reconstruction would be met. He talked a good game, reassuring them that he was exactly what the Finchon needed. At the same time, he also opened a bar on the other side of town which he christened The Lionfish Lounge. Karl hoped to compete with Donald Bickley's strip club, sans girls. Karl never liked Donald -- not him or his redneck family.

Bickley knew Karl, or rather knew *of* him. Donald had at least fifteen years on him, but still hated the man. He hated the way Karl acted, as if he was better than everyone else and that his shit was fragrant. He watched as this punk kid grew up into a regular vulture, preying on the sick and infirm with sales scams. Karl would keep an eye on the local papers and scuttle in at the last minute, buying up estates or old cars or in the case of the Finchon, a business. He didn't care for anything he purchased; he simply wanted control. Economically, Badfish was becoming somewhat of a Potter's field, drifting into a downward spiral. Once Karl took over the Finchon, the drift picked up speed and turned into a corkscrew from hell.

The motel had once been the epitome of a tourist destination. The three story building was built in 1960 and featured the classic look of the era, right down to the oversized green Chevron on the motel's highway sign. Each letter of the name F-I-N-C-H-O-N was encapsulated in a large fluorescent diamond shape. Originally, the brick foundation was painted in tones of flamingo pink and powder blue. Over the years, the colors faded, the paint chipped and peeled away, and a handful of roof shingles had started to disintegrate. A few still lay scattered on the ground, broken and untouched since the day they had fallen.

Large picture windows emphasized cement outcroppings and lined the front and back of the motel. Balconies that once supported the visiting elite now stood empty and decrepit. Cracked syringes with blood-coated needles pointed at each other on the asphalt decks. Crushed beer cans and partially filled stainless steel flasks surrounded the drug paraphernalia like a crowd gathered around street performers.

The windows that still retained curtains were broken or shattered; some of them were streaked with human filth. The bare windows were covered by sun baked newspapers, or in some cases, torn strips of mismatched clothing. Inside, pale green carpet lined the cramped wood paneled hallways. Each door led to a boxy room that had either a single bed, two double beds, or for a slightly higher price, a queen size bed.

Upon entering a room, occupants would be drenched in a haze of aquamarine with notes of stale Ajax, though the cleanliness was superficial at best. On closer inspection, one would discover waterlogged wallpaper, asbestos-laden paint flakes and a cracked ceiling. The mattresses, once immaculate, were now riddled with chew holes and non-decipherable stains. The tubs were coated in an oily slime, thankfully hidden by discolored shower curtains. Thin and incomplete sets of towels sat on racks next to the bathroom sink. Some of the toilets didn't have lids anymore, but most of the rooms at least had the flush handle.

The pool had now been relegated to the lowly position of being an oversized garbage dump. Instead of clean chlorinated water, the monstrous hole was filled with broken beer bottles, crumpled fast food bags and a smattering of mice. The overhead lights had been shot out a few years back, leaving tiny glass shards to cover the mountain of filth.

Karl Demetris, the reigning owner for the past eight years, was a diminutive, olive skinned, greasy haired creature. He was pushing forty-six but dressed more like a twenty-year old club dancer from the disco era. Sporting silky polyester shirts open practically to his waist, he wore no less than three gold medallions at a time, which usually included a large crucifix that his grandmother sent him from Greece years ago.

Leonard Mill, Karl's full-time assistant for the past few years, had just celebrated his sixty- eighth birthday. A few fishing buddies got together and planned the surprise dinner complete with his favorite cake - lemon cream - over at the Howard Johnson's, which was about fifteen miles away in Freemont. Fortunately for everyone involved, Phil Gentry had been out of town during the planning stages. Otherwise, he would have spilled the beans to Leonard within a matter of minutes. Phil loved to dabble in gossip during his thirty plus years at the plant with Leonard, but since he retired, he could now give this hobby of his some serious time and effort. Even if he had ratted out the party plans to his best friend, it wouldn't have spoiled things much. Leonard's hearing aids only worked half the time anyway.

▲ ▲ ▲

Karl arrived early to work on Monday morning. He drove his cherry red Aston-Martin into the space closest to the office door, the one reserved for Employee of the Month. The moniker was an ironic joke. Ever since the last two remaining housekeepers quit three years ago, the only employees left were Karl, Leonard and Neil, a teen-aged kid who worked part time. Like most things around the Finchon, Karl never got around to having the sign removed.

He exited his car, locked it up and walked to the front door of the office. He was fumbling for his keys when a tall, thin vagrant approached him from behind.

"Mister, got any change on ya? I need somethin' to eat."

"Get outta here. Can't you see?" he barked and pointed to an aged cardboard sign in the window. "No loitering."

"But I'm stayin' here in room 115. Hey, when are you gonna fix the TV? I'm missin' my shows."

"Why don't you go back to your room and stop hanging out in front of the office?" Karl snapped.

He turned the key, slipped inside the door and pulled it closed behind him. The man on the other side of the glass put his face and hands against the door and mumbled incoherently. Karl gestured for him to back off, which he eventually did, leaving a nasty smudge of bodily fluids and grime on the window as a reminder of his visit.

Karl shook his head. He hated a drugged up transient even more than a homeless person squatting in one of the vacant rooms. At least the homeless made an effort to stay quiet and never asked him for anything. The tenants were another story. Time and schedules and rules meant absolutely nothing to them. It was like being in charge of a bunch of toddlers, all whining and bitching and pulling at your shirt tails all day long. The only difference between them was that instead of demanding oatmeal and blankets, *these* assholes begged for money so they could buy more shit in order to stay high.

Leonard stepped around the corner of the building and practically skipped through the door, catching Karl off guard.

"Howdy, Karl. How's today treatin' you so far?"

"Leonard, what the hell are you doing here so early? It's only five past eight."

"Heck, I would have thought you'd be jumping for joy 'cause I made it here on time today. Truth is, my son an' daughter-in-law bought me one of those new-fangled alarm clocks. You know the kind where it sounds like a siren from a fire truck, EEE-OH-EEE-OH. Loud enough to wake the dead outta their eternal sleep, I tell ya. Scared the piss outta me this mornin', but heck if I didn't make it here right on time. You ought to get yourself one of those jobbers. I guarantee you'll never be late for anything again."

His boss acknowledged the story with a nod and a mild grunt and closed the door to his personal office. There were business calls to make and since Leonard was actually here and could watch the service desk, Karl wouldn't have to sit around wasting time.

A little while later, as Karl was thumbing through a stack of papers, he heard some sort of commotion coming from the outer office. For the briefest of moments, he was concerned but then caught himself. He remembered telling Leonard: *Unless something's on fire, don't interrupt me when I'm in here with the door shut.*

He ignored the distraction and picked up the phone.

"Hey, it's Karl," he said, quietly. "Look, I've had some rooms open up. Yeah, it's been pretty calm, considering how things were last month. Uh-huh, sure. How about 5:30 today? Great, see you then."

As he made cryptic notations on a yellow legal pad, Leonard burst through the door.

"Karl, I tried to stop him but he insisted on..."

"Damn it, Leonard. How many times have I explained to you not to barge in here? Is something on fire? 'Cause if it is..."

Karl didn't get the chance to finish his sentence because a skeleton of a man appeared in his doorway. He stood 6'6" with his bare arms dangling by his sides - both of which were riddled with track marks. Two half empty syringes stuck out of each median- cubital vein, the site from where most healthy people would donate blood. Fluorescent orange fluid dripped from each injection site as the man walked further into the room. His face was distended and swollen as if someone had used his head as a punching bag for the last two hours. He headed straight for Karl.

"You are a son of a bitch and I'm gonna fuckin' kill you for this," the giant spat at Karl, who was now using his chair like a buttress between himself and this monster of a man.

"Look, I don't know what you're talking about. I've done nothing except provide you with a place to stay."

"That's horseshit. Look at what your fuckin' garbage is doing to me. *I'm a freak.* It's only been twenty minutes and it's getting worse. What are you gonna do about it, you sorry asshole?"

"Hey, you don't need to be name callin', mister. You're not even supposed to be back here," Leonard chimed in.

"I got this," Karl stated. "Why don't you go on out front and keep an eye on things, alright?"

"Sure, boss."

Leonard shrugged his shoulders and closed the office door as gingerly as possible. He was actually pretty relieved to be out of there. Over the past few years, he had been witness to a number of confrontations between his boss and an unhappy client, but he quickly realized that the best side of the door to be on was the side that Karl wasn't. He did, however, place his ear against the door in the hope that he might be able to glean a word or two from either man.

"Now look," Karl started, "don't go blaming me for what you fucks shoot up into your own bodies. Every time you stick a fuckin' needle in your arm, you're the ones playing Russian roulette. I'm not forcing anyone to do anything, so why don't you do both of us a favor; get the hell out of my face, go back to your room and don't come around here again."

The junkie, whose name was Eldon, stared at Karl without as much as a blink. He didn't move when Karl yelled at him. He didn't even flinch as Karl picked up the phone and threatened to call the police.

"What are you waiting for, man? Go on! Get out of here! Did you suddenly go deaf or something?"

Then, as if in slow motion, Eldon began to break apart. His arms, still home to the syringes with brightly colored liquid oozing from them, fell to the ground. His left arm hit first with a sickening thud that would haunt Karl later that evening when he pounded back shots of upper shelf tequila by himself in his Jacuzzi. The right arm dropped next, flopping out of Eldon's shoulder socket without as much fanfare as the other one. The syringe cracked as it hit the floor. Little droplets of orange goo splattered in a geometric pattern near Karl's desk.

Eldon's left leg shook for a second before it unhinged itself from his hip and slid out from his body. Just as the right leg began its descent to the floor, what was left of Eldon fell straight down. The last thing to disengage from his body was his swelled head. Karl heard the 'pop' sound right before the disembodied head lolled from the neck over to where he stood, as he watched this horror take place right before his eyes. He saw in grotesque detail how the man's head had come off and made a beeline to his feet, as if to make one final point of contention. Karl gasped, more in disgust than anything else. He called out for Leonard.

"What is it, Karl?" Leonard opened the door slowly.

"You need to clean up…," Karl began and then screamed. "The fucker bit me!"

He raised his leg, complete with Eldon's head attached by a mouth of rotted teeth covered in orange foam and spittle, and shook it as hard as he could. The head bounced off the corner of the desk, rolled for a few seconds and landed near a fake potted plant under the window.

CHAPTER 3

LEONARD

▲ ▲ ▲

"I PROMISE I'LL BE HOME before you have supper on the table. The boss needs me to stick around. Well…," Leonard moved the receiver to his other hand, "there's still a lot of cleaning to do. Yes, dear. You know that's part of the job. But…that's because I'm getting paid to do it. At home, there's no paycheck!"

He winked at Karl who rolled his eyes and gestured for him to end the call. "Okay, I gotta get going. See you then, dear. Bye, now."

"Why do you tell her what we're doing?" Karl snapped. He handed the mop back to Leonard and took a seat at his desk. The orange liquid had already dried underneath Eldon's scattered body parts, but Karl still stepped over each of them in an exaggerated fashion to avoid contact.

"Oh, it's fine. Nothing to worry about. She was just giving me the business about cleaning *here* when I don't do much of it at home. That idea snagged her hose a bit, I'd say."

"Look," Karl said, gripping the phone's receiver in his hand. "The less everyone else knows about what goes on around here, the better. When you finish mopping up, take the pickup over to the salvage yard and get rid of…that mess. That…shit is beginning to stink."

"Will do. Say, Karl…are you going to tell me what happened in here?"

"Shush, I'm on the phone," Karl whispered as he punched at the numbered buttons.

Leonard continued his clean-up detail, traipsing back and forth between the sink in the supply room and the remnants of Eldon. He repeatedly filled the mop bucket with clean, warm water and dumped out muddied fluorescent goo. By the time he finished his fourth lap, Karl ended his call.

"I need to go out for a while. Lock the office but leave a window open when you leave. And don't let anyone bullshit you into coming back in here. We need to air this place out for a few hours."

"I understand. I'll lock up good and tight when I'm done and be back to watch the desk after lunch."

"Alright, good enough. See you tomorrow…*on time* again, right?"

Leonard laughed and gave a quick wave. He always tried to see a person's good points, though in Karl's case they were few and far between.

At sixty-eight, Leonard should have been retired long ago. After working over twenty-five years at the tire plant over in Hillman, the state screwed him and forty-five other employees from a chunk of their pensions with a legal loophole that a team of New York lawyers could barely understand. Leonard and his wife, Gertie, considered it a blessing when he was able to find work at the Finchon motel. The pay didn't come close to what he was making at the plant, but it was an income, and it supplemented things just enough to make life comfortable. Most importantly, they were still able to spoil the grandkids in the manner in which they had become accustomed.

They had always lived in Badfish. And though they watched it go from an upstanding community with good schools and plenty of jobs to a derelict, down-trodden area with more For Sale signs in yards than children in the streets, he and his wife of forty years never considered moving. This was where they grew up, got married and raised their family. The three Mill children were brought up to be strong Methodists and hard workers, just like their parents. They were all going to continue the tradition of celebrating birthdays and holidays around the dining room table, adding extra leaves to widen it in order to accommodate as many places as needed. No matter how bad things got, Leonard and Gertie had each other and a place to call home.

Once he finished, Leonard brought the mop and bucket back to the supply room and headed to the office. He shut the lights off and locked up before hoisting the laundry bags of limbs and Eldon parts out to the pickup, which was parked out back. The bags were heavy so he had to lift them into the bed of the truck one at a time. As he pushed the third bag over the lip of the truck, he heard a voice behind him.

"Hey, man. What'cha doing with all those laundry bags?"

"Uh, nothing. Machine inside is broke, so I'm just running these down to the Laundromat. But don't you worry about anything. You'll get your towels and sheets come first of the week, just like always."

"Okay. Just some weird shit going on around here these days. I'm just trying to look out for myself. Somebody's gotta."

"You'll get everything you need. Karl makes sure of that, doesn't he?"

"Yeah. He does…," the man mumbled as he fumbled with a loose button on his shirt.

Leonard climbed into the driver's seat and slammed the door shut. He waved his hand out the window before he pulled away. The man, who continued to bobble from one leg to another, waved back as he stared at the bed of the truck. His mouth dropped open. He blinked a few times, *hard*.

He couldn't be certain, but he thought he saw a hand waving from the back of the truck as well.

CHAPTER 4
KARL'S FIRST MEETING

▲ ▲ ▲

KARL DROVE HIS ASTON-MARTIN INTO the parking lot of the Lionfish Lounge, pulling directly into the designated handicap spot closest to the front door.

What am I gonna do, call the cops on myself? he would joke with Tracy, the bartender. *I own the fuckin' place and I'm going to park wherever the hell I want.*

He was already paying off local law enforcement to look the other way regarding a number of other violations at the lounge, as well as at the Finchon. When Tracy asked what she should say if a customer complained, Karl said 'tell 'em management will take it under advisement.'

"And while you're at it," he loved to add, "give 'em the finger. Under the counter, of course."

Karl spotted Tracy, who was behind the bar chatting up the Monday afternoon regulars at the bar.

"I'll be in my office, Trace. When Manny gets here, send him on back."

"Sure. Do you want…," she started to say as the office door slammed shut, "…something to drink? Okay, guess not," Tracy shrugged half-heartedly. It wasn't the first time her boss shut the door on her in mid-sentence and it probably wasn't going to be the last. She started cutting up oranges and limes for the bar buckets and continued conversing with the smattering of patrons.

Karl's office at the Lionfish wasn't much bigger than the one he had at the Finchon, but both were furnished with a large mahogany desk with locked drawers and hidden secrets. From the beginning, he kept one set of books in case of audits and another set for his private affairs. He unlocked the lower right hand drawer, bypassed a number of file folders, and mumbled something about tainted shipments and how someone's head was going to roll. He stopped at a folder marked *Incidentals* written in bright orange marker and threw it on top of the desk. The squeak of a creaky door hinge followed by a quiet knock startled him.

"Karl? Hey man, what's going on? This isn't like you, calling a meeting in the middle of the day like this."

"Come in, Manny. We have a problem."

Two men in their mid-twenties walked into the lounge and took seats at the bar. One of the men sported a buzz cut, was clean shaven and very physically fit – a spitting image from the cover of a <u>Guns and Ammo</u> magazine. The other man's appearance was quite the opposite, with a putrid scent to go with it. His clothes were one step away from rags and he was covered in sweaty slime. Tracy could smell him the second he walked through the door.

"Hi, guys. You look like you've had a rough day. Can I get you something to drink?" Tracy forced a smile and kept her hands away from her nose and mouth. She didn't want to appear impolite.

The military-looking man spoke up. "I'll take whatever's on tap."

"Great. And for you sir?"

The smelly man started to shake.

"Are you alright? Would you like me to get you some water?"

The smelly man coughed; orange droplets sprayed over the top of the bar. The counter captured most of what he expelled, but the wooden bowl of peanuts took a bit of a hit, too.

"Oh, God," Tracy grimaced. "I'm sorry, but I think you need to leave." She looked at the military man for some answers. "What's going on with your friend?"

"Ma'am, I don't know this guy. He just walked in at the same time I did. I was coming from the bus station and he happened to be walking in the same direction." He held his hands up in front of him – a motion that let her know he didn't want to get involved. Without another word, he took his beer and moved over to a stool the end of the bar.

Tracy sighed. While working at the Lionfish for over three years, she had seen her share of drunks and wise guys, but this was different. She thought about getting Karl to deal with this, but then thought better of it. *Nothing's on fire and that door is closed. I can handle this myself.*

"Okay, look. I'm really sorry but I can't have you coughing all over my bar. It's not sanitary and it's really pretty gross. You need to leave. I mean, if you're that sick, I can call an ambulance for you."

The smelly man looked up at her and parted his lips as if to speak. But instead of words, his tongue slid out of his mouth and rested between himself and Tracy like a sunbather by a pool. Tracy screamed.

In the office, Karl and Manny jumped simultaneously. The shriek from down the hall penetrated the walls and sent shivers up spines.

"Jesus, now what?" Karl said as he stood up from his chair. "Wait here. I better go see what the fuck is going on out there." He yanked the door open and yelled toward the bar. "What's wrong, Tracy?"

"Karl!"

He stomped down the hallway and into the main room where he found Tracy covering her mouth with both hands. She was pressed up against the back of the bar, distancing herself from the smelly man as much as she could.

The man was sitting on his stool and petting his tongue as it lounged on top of the counter. The only traces left of the military man were a partially empty glass of beer and two crinkly dollar bills. Everyone else had disappeared as well.

"Shit. Manny, get out here! I'm going to need some help."

CHAPTER 5

ROOM 303

▲ ▲ ▲

BOBBY PRICE WAS A TWENTY-TWO year old high school graduate who had been down on his luck ever since he left his parents' house at seventeen. He managed to squeak by during his school years; by charisma and perseverance rather than good grades. Since then, he managed to make ends meet by working odd jobs and picking up some part-time bouncer hours at Bickley's strip joint.

Although housing in Badfish had never been on what realtors might refer to as *the high end*, Bobby couldn't afford a place of his own. When sleeping on friends' couches and crashing on acquaintances' floors had started to wear thin, he realized he had to find another option, even if that meant someplace disgusting. He ended up living at the Finchon for the monthly fee of $150. In return for his hard earned money, he was given a room with a bed, clean linens once a week and a shower that worked if all the right pipes cooperated. It's not where he wanted to be, but he knew things could be a lot worse.

Lately, he had been hoping to ask Veronica, one of the dancers at the strip club, out on a date. In order to make a good impression, he had saved up a sizeable wad of cash so he could afford to take her to The Sea Grass, the most expensive restaurant in Coral Creek.

The Sea Grass, a fine dining establishment about thirty minutes north of Badfish, had quite the reputation throughout the county. It was one of the few places that prided itself on its white table cloths, tapered candles, and snooty waiters - the kind that carried around a little scraping knife to clean wayward crumbs after each course. Bobby imagined that Veronica would enjoy a place like that, especially after having to work in a dump like Bickley's.

He sat on his bed scribbling numbers into a notebook, trying to figure out a way to get some extra cash when he heard a knock on his door.

"Come in."

"Hey, man, 'sup? Haven't seen you for a few days."

"Yeah, I know. I'm putting in some extra hours at Bickley's. Kinda low on cash these days an' I'm trying to save up for some stuff."

"Yeah...yeah, I feel ya."

The man who Bobby knew only as G-Force helped himself to the rest of the cheese and crackers that were on the counter next to a crumpled up tee-shirt. G grabbed a chair, turned it around and straddled it, dropping crumbs and pieces of cellophane wrapper onto the dirty carpet.

"This is good…you got any more of these?" He tossed the remainder of the wrapper on the floor and brushed his hands against his stained grey sweatpants.

"Uh, no I don't. That was actually the rest of my dinner."

"Oh, geez, man, sorry 'bout that," G-Force said as he eyed the rest of the room for rogue food stuffs. "Jus' hungry, I guess. But, hey, the reason I came by? Karl got some shit in last night. *Good* stuff, you dig? Only cost you a dub."

"Thanks, but I gotta pass. There's this girl…," Bobby started to explain, but thought better about sharing too many details. He didn't trust anyone too much at the Finchon, especially with details of his life.

"Oh, yeah?" G-Force smiled a big, toothy grin and held his hand up waiting for Bobby to meet his high-five. "I didn't know you had lady, Bobby. Hey, if everything goes well, don't forget about *me*. Maybe you can hook me up with someone from the club, too. But, uh, yeah, I see where your head is at. Well, when you're ready to make a little green, you just find me an' I'll set you up."

"Thanks, man, I'll do that. I gotta get back to this, okay? I'll see you later."

"Later, my man," G-Force said. "You know where to find me, right? 317."

"Yep, I got it. Thanks again."

He watched his door close. A moment later, Bobby could hear G-Force knocking on Room 301. *Good luck with that guy,* he thought. No one had seen anyone come or go from that room for over a week. The last time Bobby *had* seen him, the guy looked like death warmed over; gaunt, toothpick thin, and track marks all over his body. If a new tenant had moved in, under the radar so to speak, during the past few days, Bobby wouldn't have been surprised. That was the one sure thing about living at the Finchon — sometimes people just disappeared and new ones took their place.

CHAPTER 6

BICKLEY

▲ ▲ ▲

DONALD BICKLEY LEANED UP AGAINST the bar with a Pabst long neck in one hand and his balls in the other. Between the low lighting of the strip club and his body angle, no one could say with certainty if he was fondling himself while he watched the girls on stage or not. Even if anyone had noticed, no one worth their salt would dare say anything.

Over the course of his sixty-plus years, he had probably fought with every man in Badfish, either by fisticuffs or a screaming match. Years ago, a bunch of kids from his old high school snuck into his house to scare him. Instead, they caught Donald in his mom's yellow sun dress with the skirt hiked up around his naked buttocks, waiting for one of his brothers. Things were never quite the same after that.

As a businessman, he faced strong opposition and resistance when he initially applied to get a license to open up a strip club. Back in the late-seventies, there were a lot of families with small children and even more religious naysayers, but Donald's mind was made up. Opening a strip club would prove that he *wasn't any fuckin' pansy ass* and as long as women were willing to dance, then by God, he was going to provide a place for them. With no wife or kids of his own, there were still plenty of musings around town about Donald's sexuality.

As a younger man, Donald used his fists against the bastards who started any ugly gossip. But as he got older, he replaced punching and fistfights with cuss words and strings of vulgarity. *So what if he had never been with a woman? He was no fag and that was for damn sure.* And if he had to fuck over everyone in Badfish to prove it, that was just fine with him. However, the constant drain of having to defend himself for so long was getting tiresome. Anger turned into depression. Depression turned into unyielding loneliness. Then Nina walked into his life.

Nina Dumont was onstage now, grinding out dance moves to World Party's 1986 hit "Ship of Fools." She was Donald's favorite – young and slender with long, black hair down to her waist. For this performance, she wore a short, black cabaret corset with a satin bow tie and top hat. The cane in her hand was just a prop but it was obvious to Donald that she was well versed in using it for other purposes.

After a sultry two minute intro, Nina finally made eye contact with Donald. She rubbed herself and opened her mouth wide; her tongue searched for a willing hole. If she was close enough to touch his face and enter between his dry lips at that moment, he would have fainted.

He kneaded his groin area hard and fast. If anyone had been seated at the bar, the situation would have been screamingly obvious. He moaned and grunted and splashed his beer until foam spurted over the lip of the bottle. At the height of the final chorus swell, Nina grabbed her ears and pulled down as hard as she could, raising her face to the ceiling and let out a cry of exhilaration. That's all Donald needed to see. At that same moment, he released his own passion down the front of his trousers. A warm, sticky stream ran from his crotch, down both pant legs, and pooled on the wooden floor.

When Donald regained his composure, he set what was left of his beer on the counter and went into the bathroom to clean up. When he returned, Nina was seated at the bar waiting for him. She wore a robe over what was left of her costume and sipped from a glass of red wine.

"Mr. Bickley, do you have a minute? I need to talk to you about something."

Donald wiped his face with his handkerchief and straddled the bar stool next to hers. "Sure I have time. Especially for *you*, Nina."

She smiled. She knew that he liked her and because of that, she also knew exactly what buttons to push.

"Well, I hate to ask you this but me and a few of the other girls are having problems making our rent this month. We can't stay in our apartment an' the landlord is giving us until the end of the week to come up with money. And you know how slow it's been around here lately."

"Are you wanting more hours?"

"Uh, well, either that or...do you know where we can stay? I know a couple of the girls live at the Finchon. They say it only costs..."

"No, not there," Donald countered. Even the *name* of the place conjured up a mental image of Karl Demetris, the asshole who continued to perpetuate the ugly rumors against him. "That place isn't safe. I don't want you staying there even one night. Here, come on back to my office and let me see what I can do."

Donald stood up and helped Nina off her stool. She followed him to his office and plopped down on the couch near a mini-fridge. She watched him as he scooted behind his desk and reach into his shirt pocket. He pulled a tiny key out and crouched down so she could barely see his comb-over. When he reappeared from behind the desk, he held a hefty roll of cash in his fist. Nina's face lit up as she gasped. She had never seen that much money in one place before.

"There's two thousand dollars in this bundle. You take it and get yourself and your friends into a decent place, you hear me? This should be more than enough to cover you for a while. Will this help?"

Nina took the money from Donald, feeling the weight of the cash. She wanted to smell it; fresh minted bills from the bank, still banded. Her eyes stared at the pile in her hands.

"Yeah, this...this should help."

"If anyone else was askin', I'd tell 'em to fuck off. But since it's you...," Donald mumbled and looked at the floor. "Now, go and find yourself a nice place to live. I don't want to see you back here until you do, understand?"

"Yes, Mr. Bickley. I'll start looking for a new place tomorrow."

Nina popped up off the couch and skittered to the door. "Thanks again. This is a huge help."

Donald heard her dash down the hall; five inch heels clicking as she ran. He leaned back in his chair, closed his eyes and gently massaged his penis through the damp spot on his pants. With his other hand, he gently pulled on his left ear lobe.

CHAPTER 7

LEONARD'S NIGHT SHIFT

▲ ▲ ▲

ONE NIGHT A WEEK, LEONARD worked the graveyard shift at the Finchon. From 7p.m. to 5a.m., he had the laborious task of making sure no one raised too much hell. And if by some miracle an actual tourist stopped by, he was supposed to show them the *expensive* room. What that meant, as Karl explained it to Leonard, was that the room came with a two full sets of towels and the likelihood of bed bugs would be considerably lower than in the other rooms.

At 7:05pm, Leonard walked into the main office and greeted Neil, the high school kid who worked part time.

"Hey there, pal. How goes things this evening?"

"Pretty good, Mr. L. Kinda slow…as usual."

"Any trouble to speak of?"

"No, not really, 'cept this guy keeps comin' in here asking for stuff."

Leonard took his sweater off and draped it over the service desk chair while Neil collected his comic books.

"What kind of stuff?"

"I dunno. Just stuff like towels and cups. You know, things like that."

"Hmm, is that so?" Leonard said.

"Yeah. I didn't think it was a big deal. I mean, the guy was nice enough. Well, I'm outta here. See ya later, Mr. L."

"Not if I see you first, buddy boy!" he snickered back as he gave his young charge a friendly salute.

The first few hours tended to be slow; the regulars wandering in to drop off rent money or filing the usual complaint about something not working in their room. But Leonard didn't mind. It helped pass the time and it was nice to have someone to chat with, even if they were just blowing off steam.

He hoisted himself up onto the chair Neil had warmed and pulled the Daily Post from his satchel. He turned to the sports section. His buddy Phil had gone on and on about how some guy hooked a fifty pound mud cat over in Stillsville. Leonard called *hogwash* on the story and reminded Phil that there hadn't been that big of a catch within a hundred mile radius in over sixty years. Besides being the town gossip, Phil was the master of the tall tale. Everyone in Badfish knew him as the 'town crier.' When he retired, people joked that they wouldn't need to subscribe to the local paper anymore. All they had to do for news was call Phil Gentry.

"Leonard," Phil had told him, "I'm as serious as a heart attack. Go down to Goody's and pick up today's paper and look at the bottom of section D4 if you don't believe me. I tell you, as sure as I'm standing here right in front of you, that son-of-a-bitch caught one *this big.*" He was holding his hands as far apart as he could manage.

"I might do just that," Leonard smirked as he poked Phil good-naturedly in the shoulder.

Leonard folded his paper in half and held it close to the desk lamp to get a better look at the article.

"Well, I'll be...," he chuckled, "here it is, right where he said it was. Fifty-one pounds and ten ounces. That'll make one hell of a fish fry."

The bell above the office door tinkled. Leonard raised his head and set the paper down.

"Why, hello there. What can I help you with tonight?"

"I-I need a few more towels."

"Okay. What room are you in? I'll bring 'em over for ya."

"No. No..., I-I can carry them myself."

"Hey, it's no problem. I don't mind the walk over on a nice night like this. What room are you in?"

"I-I just need them *now,* okay? I can take them *myself.*"

"Sure. Sure, pal. Give me just a minute, alright? I gotta get 'em from the supply room."

Leonard got up, took a set of keys off the wall and went into the back. As he fished around for a complete set of towels, he tried to make small talk with the impatient man.

"So, uh, tell me. How long have you been staying with us?"

The young man didn't respond.

"Is this your first fall at the Finchon?"

Still no answer.

Leonard tried a different tactic.

"Here we go. Found one of each; bath, hand, washcloth and even a mat. You know, I really like this time of year, don't you? Yes sir, early fall is my favorite time of year," he said as he walked back to the service counter. "Don't you just love how the trees turn all kinds of colors and the weather has a bit of a bite to it? Now, me, I love fishing, so you'd think that I'd pick summer for my favorite, but nope, you'd be wrong, my friend. I'm partial to fall. Oh, that's probably because my wife and I married in mid-September. You know, after you've been with someone for so long, I think you tend to start liking the same things, even if you didn't like 'em at first. What about you, partner? You got someone special?"

The nervous man stared wordlessly at Leonard. He managed a slight nod and held out his hands for the towels. Leonard continued the one-sided conversation, interpreting his nod as an affirmative answer and a signal to continue.

"Good for you, having someone special. Sure makes tough times go a bit easier, don't it? Where's this little lady from, if you don't mind me asking?" Still, the young man said nothing, but reached for the pile of clean towels that Leonard was still holding. "Oh, blasted. I didn't mean to bend your ear. Here ya go, pal. Now, if you'd be good enough to tell me what room you're staying in, I'll make a note for Karl. For some crazy reason, he likes to keep track of these things."

"303".

"Three-oh-three -- got it. Well, you have a good night, okay?"

Leonard didn't expect to get a response, so he was surprised when Bobby Price uttered the word 'thanks'.

▲ ▲ ▲

The hours passed slowly. Leonard filled his time with crossword puzzles, reading, and collecting the occasional rent deposit. The phone rang only once; a family inquiring about the cost of a couple of rooms. He cheerfully told them a little about the motel and then added what he thought was the real selling point - that a one night stay would cost only $54. The man on the other end of the line thanked him but declined the offer to make a reservation. After losing what might have been an actual customer, Leonard snuck into the supply room and settled down on a rollaway cot for a short nap. When the bell above the office door woke him from a fishing dream, his watch read 4:30a.m.

"Just a minute. I'll be out there in a jiff."

Leonard rubbed his eyes and tucked in his shirt.

"Alright, now, what can I -," he stopped mid-sentence after seeing the person standing at the counter.

"I-I need some towels."

"Now, listen here, guy. I try to be a good sport about all this here, but something's beginning to smell a little fishy to me. I remember you comin' in at the start of my shift asking for that very same thing. You wanna tell me the real story about what's going on here?"

"I-I need more towels…for the bathroom. I lost the other ones."

Leonard rubbed the side of his face with his hand and took a deep breath. He was all too familiar with the peculiar things that went on at the motel, things he didn't want to know about if push came to shove. But now he was feeling a little too involved. This guy was behaving like a cat caught with its paw on the pet guinea pig. Leonard didn't want any part of whatever trouble was brewing in Room 303 by providing extra linens or anything else.

"Why don't you just come back a little later this morning when Karl's here? Then the two of you can decide what to do about those disappearing towels, okay?"

Bobby Price stared at Leonard for the briefest of moments, then turned around and walked out. Leonard followed him from the office and watched as the young man crossed the parking lot and headed back to his room. He saw him unlock the door and enter, but right before shutting it, a soiled orange-spotted hand towel sailed out across the balcony and landed close to the other towels. The discarded linens formed a rather pretty mosaic pattern in the center of the gravel lot.

CHAPTER 8

ROOM 303

▲ ▲ ▲

G-FORCE DIDN'T BOTHER ACKNOWLEDGING THE superfluous greeting and explanation from Bobby when he came back empty handed. Instead, the moment he entered the room, G tossed another crumpled towel out and went back to his amateur science lab. A tiny rusted burner that was practically falling apart from age was working hard to heat a bubbling mixture in a small bowl. He stirred it carefully with a corroded spoon.

Bobby gazed at the assortment of paraphernalia that surrounded G-Force: tubes, hoses, syringes, dark brown bottles, and a pile of eye droppers. G started singing to himself in order to help him focus on the task at hand. Bobby shook his head, turned on the television and sat on his bed.

"You about done?"

"Relax, man. Good shit takes time."

"I gotta tell you, G; I don't like you doing all that stuff in here. Why can't you do it in your own room?"

"Hang on…hang…on. Jus' one more thing here…and… there. Shake and bake, my man. Let this cool down for another few minutes and bam! We got ourselves enough to score some *real* dough."

"*Real* dough?"

"Thousands, man. Peeps pay a pretty penny for *shit,* but only if it's good. Karl said we can cook it up on our own, or if we didn't want to go to the trouble, he has some that's premade. I just like to do it myself, you know?"

"Yeah," Bobby said. He flipped through the same eleven channels of basic cable; one of the special perks of living at the Finchon. "But why can't you do all that in *your* room?"

"'Cause you got an empty room on one side and Beefy Boy on the other. An' everyone knows that Beefy Boy is cool. I don't trust *my* neighbors. Your room is like a safe house."

"Well, I don't wanna get caught with all that shit in *my* room when I'm not even using it. Hell, I'm not even *selling* it. You know, that old dude in the office was pressing me pretty hard about all the extra towels."

"It's cool, man. Just be cool. I can't help spilling some shit. It's like a big chemistry lab, you know? Fuck 'em anyway. They got enough of those cheap ass towels for the whole fuckin' place and then some. You see what Karl drives every day? He can afford to give those towels away and not think a lick about it."

"I can't get kicked out of here, man. I mean I'm saving up, but its slow going, you know?"

"That can change, bro," G-Force said as he held up the mixing bowl.

G took a syringe, filled it with the phosphorescent orange liquid and pressed the plunger a fraction of a millimeter. A large drop squeezed itself out and hung on the top and side of the needle. Bobby couldn't turn away. It was as if he could hear the droplet whisper, tempting him, oozing over itself as if to wash away his sins. He tried to fight its pull, to rationalize:

It could be easy money, especially in a place like this. What if I sold it for just a little while, just long enough to save and get the hell out of here? It wouldn't have to be forever, just a couple of weeks. Maybe a couple of months. I'd stop as soon as I had enough.

"What'cha thinkin', Bobby? I can see the wheels...the gears grinding away... You're probably thinking 'bout what this sweetness is really like, is that it? Or maybe you're thinking about workin' on the business end of things? That's cool, too. I can set you up. You understand me?"

He brought a drug-filled syringe closer to Bobby's face, egging him on to hold it.

"Yeah, yeah, that's it. *Feel* that. Get to know that warm sweet love. You do know what you're feeling, right? *Money*, my man. Right there in your hand. That is the question and the answer all rolled into one. Your ticket to getting yourself out of here. That's really all you want, isn't it?"

Bobby Price met eyes with G-Force. It was beginning to feel like an offer he couldn't refuse.

CHAPTER 9

TRACY

▲ ▲ ▲

TRACY WELSH STEPPED OUT OF a hot shower and grabbed a towel off the door hook. She wrapped it around her shoulders and dried her hair with the frayed ends. It felt good not to have to rush this morning. Kyle had given her two days off in a row, something that didn't happen very often, so she wanted to enjoy every minute of them.

Tracy graduated from college with a degree in philosophy and a heart full of lofty ambition a little over three and a half years ago. Instead of securing a high paying position, she ended up with a piece of paper that wasn't worth much in the eyes of potential employers, and a pile of debt. With her proverbial tail between her legs, she went back to her parents' home, listened to the requisite *we told you to major in something that would get you a job, not help explore your inner feelings* lectures, and proceeded to set up a make-shift bedroom in the basement. Her options for living comfortably in her parents' home were pretty limited. Her younger brother had taken over her room while she was at school and *his* bedroom had been turned into Mrs. Welsh's scrapbook nook.

When online job hunting proved to be nothing but an exercise in filling out standardized forms, Tracy realized that finding substantial employment was going to take longer than she initially thought. In the meantime, she applied for a bartending position at the Lionfish Lounge and promised herself that the job would be temporary – *very* temporary. She thought of it as a last resort, a ditch effort until she landed something in her field. But three years later, she knew all the regulars by name, was placing weekly stock orders, and was the official *go to* person for the rest of the small staff.

She finished drying her hair and tossed the towel into the clothes basket. One reprieve of living with the parents – Mom did the laundry. Tracy helped with some cooking and cleaning, but thankfully, Mom kept the task of laundry all to herself.

"The last thing your father needs is pink socks or underwear. You'd never hear the end of it. Heck, *no one* would hear the end of it," Tracy's mom told her the day she moved back home. That was, of course, inserted between the '*I told you so*' speeches about her choice of college degree.

With her parents at work and her brother in school, the entire house was hers for the day. She fixed breakfast, put the pans in the sink and sat at the kitchen table. The remote, left in the middle of the counter where her dad had put it from the night before was just out of reach.

"Shit," she muttered. She leaned over as far as she could and almost knocked her cell phone to the floor. She caught it in mid-air and on the first ring.

"Hello?"

"Tracy? Wow, girl, I'm kind of surprised you're up already. I was just going to leave you a message about tonight."

"Veronica?"

"Who else do you know that would be calling this early in the morning? No one with a *day* job, that's for sure. Hell, I haven't even been to bed yet."

Tracy laughed.

Tracy knew Veronica from Marsten Univeristy, having graduated in the same class and with the same major. Tracy also knew that if it weren't for the grace of God, Veronica might have ended up as the bartender and *she* would have been the one dancing at Bickley's.

"So, what's happening tonight?"

"Well, when do you get off from Lionfish? Eight? Nine?"

"I'm off for the next *two days*. Can you believe it?"

"*What?* That scum bum gave you two days off in a row? You're not blowing him under the bar, are you?"

"Shut up, V," she laughed again. "But, yeah, I'm free to-night. What's going on?"

"Well, there's this party I heard about from one of the girls at the club. It's supposed to be pretty crazy an' I thought you might want to go. I can pick you up or meet you there if that's easier."

"Where is it, in Badfish?"

"No. It's about forty-five minutes away. Right off of Petersburg Road near Coral Creek."

"Oh, okay, yeah, I know about where that's at. Why don't you just pick me up? It'll probably be easier to go in one car. Plus, it sounds like you already know the way."

"Great. Eight o' clock?"

"Yeah, eight is good. See you then."

CHAPTER 10

KARL'S SECOND MEETING

▲ ▲ ▲

KARL SAT IN HIS OFFICE surrounded by mountains of paperwork, reams of ledgers and crates of balance sheets. It was a bit of a challenge to keep the legitimate files separated from the bogus ones because after a while, they all started to blur together. He had one set of records for all the monthly payments and rental fees and another set marked as *extraneous fees,* the ones that weren't officially connected to the running of the motel.

Behind him towered piles of receipts. Most of these were for the maintenance work that supposedly happened over the previous years; all forged by Karl. The last time any actual work occurred was *before* Karl took it over. He would never put any money toward the business. He also made it clear to Leonard that *he* should never spearhead projects of his own either.

Karl's sole purpose for owning the Finchon was simple; make as much money as possible by using the motel as a failing business write-off. If that meant renting rooms for a pittance without having to invest real dollars back into the business, so be it. The motel was going to be a front for drug trades – that was his original plan. He never cared about the service industry. The Lionfish Lounge was more profitable from its inception and continued to be so over the years. He took better care of it, though not by much, and in turn it was patronized by regular customers as well as tourists passing through town.

Karl raised his head from the torrent of papers when he heard Manny pull up in his old, rust-coated Chevy. Karl kept after him to fix it. It was difficult if not impossible to be discreet when the sounds of a junk heap pulled into the parking lot every other week.

"About time," Karl huffed.

He opened his office door to find Leonard napping against his closed fist, arm propped up on his elbow. Karl let out an exasperated sigh, went over to the service desk and tapped Leonard on the shoulder. The touch startled him out of another fishing dream.

"Hogwash! That bait is for the birds!" He rubbed his eyes. "Oh, Karl, how are you?"

"I'm *awake*."

"Sorry, boss. Just a little tired today. Phil and the guys were over last night and I guess we stayed up too late tellin' stories. You know how it is, don'cha? One story leads right into another and before ya know it, the little woman is givin' you the eyeball with her arms crossed, standing there in her bathrobe. And if you know what's good for ya, you best hustle the guys out the back door and get upstairs to bed."

"Can't say I've had the experience."

"But you know what baffles me? It's that some of the guys remember the fishing trip we took up to the U.P. back in the fall of, oh heck, what year was that again? I wanna say it was '77, but don't quote me on that. Could 'a been '76. But I'll swear on a stack of Bibles that the fish they *say* they caught wasn't during that particular trip, but was actually on the one to Wisconsin. Huh. Maybe we ought to start writing down who caught what and where the heck we were when it happened. That would clear up some of those confounded disagreements, don't you think?"

Karl just stared at Leonard. What *he* thought was confounding was the fact that the man could speak for the better part of four minutes without taking so much as a breath.

"Leonard, could you take care of these invoice logs? I'm going to be in a meeting for a while."

"Sure. I'll get on 'em right away," Leonard answered. He picked up a hefty stack of papers.

Manny walked in and greeted the two men.

"Karl. Leonard. How are you fellas today?"

Before Leonard could start another story, Karl motioned toward the back. "Come on. I've got some numbers to show you."

"Nice to see you again, Leonard."

"You too, buddy. Stop by on your way out and I'll tell you about that new fishing line they got in at Steeley's Sports. It's a real doozy."

"*Manny?*" Karl pressed the moment as he held the office door open.

Once both men were seated, Karl didn't waste any time.

"Alright, look. I know about the change in your suppliers and how this asshole was giving you some bullshit story about losing his overseas connections or whatever, but we've got a real problem here. I've given him *and you* plenty of time to iron all this out, but I'm the one left to clean up all this fuckin' filth. Hell, just in the past, what...*month?* I've had to...well shit, you saw what happened at the Lionfish the other day. Whatever the hell he's selling to *you* is piss poor quality, but I'm the one that ends up with the dead bodies."

"I don't know what to tell you, Karl. The last time I talked to him, he swore up and down that everything's cool now. He said he's getting the stuff directly from New Orleans instead of the Ukraine and there shouldn't be any more issues. Now, uh, I can't be held responsible for any of the old stuff that's still floatin' around, if you know what I mean."

"Well, somewhere along the line, someone screwed you over, 'cause this shit's still happening. And if they're screwing *you*, they're screwing *me*, and I'm not going to put up with it. So before *we* do any more business, why don't you go test this new product on your *own* people? If they start falling apart, you can deal with it in your own backyard. In the meantime, I'm gonna make some calls, 'cause it looks like I gotta get some other irons in the fire."

"No, man, don't go to someone else, please. I need this. I mean, fuck, you're my main score. I gotta keep you on my route, man. What do you want, a lower drop? I-I can do that. I can let you have a shipment for twenty percent off your usual cost, okay?"

"You're not understanding me, Manny. I don't want to handle any more damn body parts. That is not my job, plus it eats into my revenue. Dead bodies don't buy fuckin' shit."

"I get it...I do. Let me talk to my guy again, okay? Just don't go anywhere else yet. Give me a chance to make this right. You won't have to clean up anything anymore, I promise."

Karl eyed Manny for an uncomfortably long moment. Manny looked like a bug squirming around on the faux leather chair, trying to avoid being stuck with a pin. But Karl didn't care one way or another about bodies breaking apart or transients dropping dead. What drove him was the bottom line; the profit at the end of the day. If a few punk drug addicts keeled over in the process, fuck 'em. The problem, as Karl saw it, was that *too many* were dropping dead as of late, enough to cut into profits and enough to arouse unwanted suspicion.

The thought of looking for a different supplier, as well as new tenants, *had* crossed his mind recently. Over the past few months, the Finchon had been running with half of its units vacant. Maybe it was just the weak ones being weeded out, a kind of twisted Darwinian game. If he made an effort to rent out the rest of the rooms, he could gain more than what he lost from the dead ones. Plus, the few tenants that weren't into drugs were still making the monthly payments.

"Okay. Okay, fine. I'll stick with you for a little while longer, but don't mistake this gesture for kindness. You get out there and get this shit nailed down or our next meeting is going to be our last."

"I get it, Karl. You won't have to worry about anything. You got every right to be pissed off, but the next time you see me, you'll be thanking me."

"I hope so, Manny. For your sake as well as mine."

CHAPTER 11

THE FINCHON MOTEL

▲ ▲ ▲

"So, WOULD THE ROOM JUST be for you? You mentioned a friend of yours…," Karl said, unlocking Room 301 and letting the young woman walk in ahead of him. He switched the lights on as they entered and shut the door behind them.

"Well, yeah, *this* place would be for me, but she might want her own room at some point. I gave her your phone number."

"That's wonderful, Miss Dumont."

Karl smiled and turned away for a moment to unbutton his shirt a little farther down. He turned back around and ran his hand over his slicked back hair. "You're awfully pretty to be living in a place like this. If I saw you on the street, I would've pegged you for a Coral Creek girl, for sure."

"Uh, yeah right. Not if you work at Bickley's. Now, the website said that the rent is cheap. A hundred and fifty a month and that's supposed to include a bunch of stuff."

"Absolutely. You've got a bed, dresser, table and two chairs. There's a counter if you want to bring your own microwave. Basic cable is included and just around this wall is your bathroom. You have to bring your own toiletries, but we provide towels and bed linens once a week. If you need more, just come down to the office. I'm usually there, but if not, Leonard can help you, or Neil. He's a high school kid that helps out."

"I thought the website said there was a pool."

"Uh...yeah..., it's kind of under construction right now. But...," Karl moved in closer, "if you feel the need for a dip, let me know. I've got a hot tub back at my house."

"What's that supposed to mean?"

"It means I think you're kinda pretty, and if you have any special requests, I'm your man."

"Oh? And what's the catch? You won't raise my rent?"

Karl placed his hands on her shoulders, guiding her closer to him. He bent down to her ear.

"Speaking of things rising..."

"Uh, no." Miss Dumont backed away. "I don't think so, pal. I'm just looking for a cheap place to live, not a cheap date."

"Fine, have it your way," he said as he straightened out his clothes and buttoned up his shirt. "But if you ever change your mind..."

"I doubt it."

"What about the room?"

"Yeah, I guess. It's month to month, right?"

"That's right."

They headed down the iron stairwell and walked through the parking lot. As they crossed the area, a few men sitting outside were tending to slabs of meat on tiny grills in front of their open doors. They sat on torn lawn chairs and upside down buckets; a make-shift picnic in the works. Partially empty bottles of beer and cheap whisky surrounded their feet. Behind them, the empties lay dead in a pile. The men watched Karl and the new tenant head to the main office. Some of them hooted and whistled.

"Knock it off or I'll raise your rent, you assholes," Karl shouted at the group. There was a smattering of commentary, but Miss Dumont and Karl were too far away to hear specifics.

"Does that happen often around here?"

"If those creeps give you any trouble, you tell me. They just don't see too many ladies living here...at least not ones that look as good as you do. But I won't put up with anybody harassing you," Karl lied. He had already bedded three other women tenants from the motel.

"Look, I don't want to live here if it's really *not* safe."

"Darlin', you have my word that this place is fine. Don't you listen to all those blowhards from Bickley's telling you the Finchon isn't safe, especially Donald Bickley. You have the best room in the entire motel," Karl lied again.

"What do you mean? Why *especially* Mr. Bickley?"

"Because, my dear, that man's a freak. He might be your boss, but he's a real nutjob."

"Why do you say that? I've never had any problems with him."

"That's because you're not his type. You're a woman."

As they walked into the office, Leonard woke up with a snort as the little bell above the door tinkled.

"Huh? What? Can I help you?"

"Contract, Leonard. Bring a contract into my office. Miss Dumont is going to be joining us. She's moving into Room 301."

"Oh, that's great. Welcome to the Finchon, Miss Dumont. I'm Leonard. If you need anything, you just give me a big ol' holler, alrighty?"

Miss Dumont held out her hand.

"Thanks, Leonard, but you can call me Nina."

CHAPTER 12

ROOM 303

▲ ▲ ▲

BOBBY PRICE LEANED OVER THE side of the bed, chin resting on his folded arms, intently watching as G-Force loaded up another round of syringes. G prepped thirty vials — fifteen for each of them. Over the past few weeks, it had become a ritual; G prepared the dope and Bobby pushed his portions to anyone willing to buy them. Some of the customers at Bickley's strip club learned that if they had the cash, not only could they score with the dancers but experience a hell of a high as well.

Bobby was now on the verge of making some decent money. He was taking on extra hours at Bickley's, and extra hours these days not only meant a larger paycheck but more opportunities for selling. G-Force explained that the more they sold, the more money everyone involved in the business would make. Just like a pyramid scheme; if the *up line* was happy, then everybody was happy.

"You think we got enough for tonight? I don't want to run out, man. If this party's anything like the last one, there'll be a ton of people there."

"Be cool, little dude. G's been taking care of you, right? You just go on ahead and I'll meet up with you later, dig?"

"I got it," Bobby nodded. Everything about this still made him nervous.

"Hey, uh, G? Can I ask you something?"

"Ask away. I'm right here."

"Do...do you ever use any of that stuff? I mean, I know you do other shit and that's fine, man. I'm not judging or anything. I'm just wondering if you've ever done...*that* stuff."

"This here?" G-Force held up one of the syringes. The contents glowed in the din of the room. Bobby had drawn the shades for privacy.

"No, man, I don't piss where I eat, you feel me?"

"I-I think so. But, you never tried it, not even once?"

"Shit. Look at this. You got to be fucked up in the head to squirt something like this in your arm."

"Yeah...that's kinda what I thought, too."

"Why do you ask, man? Are you looking for a hook-up yourself?"

Bobby hesitated. There was something strangely alluring about this drug. The mystery surrounding it pulled at him, taunting him. What would it be like, to feel the hot liquid fill every pore of your body, every cell pulsating with a rush never known before? He wouldn't have to do a whole vial... just a drop, maybe two. *A small taste of the mystery.* But selling it was one thing and shooting it was another. He was so close to having enough money to ask Veronica on a date, the last thing he wanted to do was to screw that opportunity up.

"Eh, I guess I'm a little curious about it, but, um, no. I don't think I wanna go down that road."

"Good man. You stick with G-Force and don't be doing any of *this* shit."

G finished filling the last syringe while Bobby stocked both of his jacket pockets with a stash of needles.

"You ready, G-man?"

"Ooh, Bobby P., I was born ready. But, I have a few stops to make first. I'll see you later, man."

Bobby grinned as he locked the door to his room and followed G downstairs to the parking lot where they parted company for a while.

PARTY TIME

▲ ▲ ▲

BY THE TIME BOBBY ARRIVED, the party was in full swing. He guessed that there must have been about a hundred people, but it was hard to say for sure. Some were milling about in the front and side yards, but most had congregated in the back. Groups of revelers were coming and going from the house itself, a rustic country two-story that had plenty of land and no neighbors; it was the perfect spot to host a large gathering.

As Bobby rounded the side of the house, he saw a large crowd surrounding a sizeable bonfire. Smaller cliques dotted areas further back, distancing themselves from the heat. At least four port-a-potties stood at one end of the yard and three large grills were stationed at the other end. Whatever was cooking smelled wonderful, making Bobby's stomach growl. A long row of beer coolers lined one side of the house. Bobby was convinced; this party *was* much larger than the last.

He spotted G-Force and waved.

"Hey G, I'm going to head inside an' see if Veronica made it. I'll catch up with you later."

"Cool, man," G answered and disappeared into the crowd that surrounded the bonfire.

Bobby walked past small enclaves of drunken girls who were slurring their words and making promises they wouldn't keep to each other or anyone else. He scooted by couples making out in the front doorway and squeezed between clusters of young men in the foyer. When he managed to break through the human barriers and enter the interior of the home, he was hit in the face with a waft of marijuana.

People were everywhere; the staircases leading up and down were practically impassible. The floor itself swelled with sweaty bodies. As he maneuvered his way into the kitchen, he spotted a familiar face.

"Veronica! Over here!" Bobby shouted and held up his hand, trying to be heard above the noise.

"Bobby!" Veronica called back. She strained to see around the people blocking her view. "Meet me out front!" She called through cupped hands and then pointed to the door.

He nodded and gave her a 'thumbs up'.

They met on the front porch, clasped hands and headed for a quiet spot in the side yard. Bobby pointed to an empty picnic bench under a row of trees. He hoisted himself up onto the tabletop while Veronica sat on one end of the bench. She stretched her legs out in front of her. They sat together quietly for a few minutes before either of them broke the silence.

"So, uh...come here often?" Bobby asked, smiling sheepishly.

Veronica laughed behind her hand. "Can't say that I do, or from the looks of it, ever will again. Do *you* know any of these people?"

"No...I, uh, was actually glad to see *you*. I don't know anybody else here except one guy from the Finchon, and to tell you the truth, I don't really even know him all that well. What about you?"

"No. I brought one of my friends to a party here the last time, but she didn't like it all that much. I don't think I'm going to stay very long myself. I kind of thought this party would be...a little different."

"Different?" Bobby asked. He put his hand in his coat pocket and felt the point of a syringe. "What do you mean?"

"Well, I guess I thought there'd be more stuff to do. Last time, when I brought my friend, there were people dancing and a bunch of wading pools and I don't know. The whole feel of it was different." She paused to think about that night. "There were just other kinds of people there that time."

"Other kinds of people? Like aliens and monsters?" he said, making a goofy face and holding his arms out in front of him like Frankenstein. She laughed and slapped his knee.

"I meant not so many drug heads, you know? Everybody here's kind of like the burn outs from high school."

He put his hands back in his pockets and stroked a syringe full of orange liquid. He felt its warmth through the glass vial and traced the outline of the needle with his thumb, fighting a powerful urge to jam it into his soft flesh and push the plunger. It could happen so quickly, no one would even know.

"Bobby?"

He closed his eyes and pictured himself naked lying on top of her, writhing together on the picnic table, syringes sticking out of their arms and legs. With each pounding thrust of their groins, their skin would rhythmically pulsate with a deeper orange hue. The liquid would ooze out of every orifice – mouths, noses, ears, eyes, anuses. At the point of their mutual climax, they would explode like glass shards shattering into the darkness, orange flecks of glowing skin and tissue twinkling airborne against the black sky.

"Bobby? Are you okay?"

His eyes flew open. "Huh? Uh, yeah. Yeah. I think the music just got to me, too. Way too loud in there, you're absolutely right about that."

"No, I said that I didn't think there would be that many druggy people. I was hoping this party would be like the last one."

"Yeah, that's what I meant."

A loud popping noise not unlike a gunshot came from the backyard, jarring Bobby and Veronica from their stilted conversation. They stopped talking and looked toward the back of the house.

"What the fuck was that? Come on," Bobby said.

He hopped off the table and held out his hand for Veronica. She took it and they ran toward the noise. As they rounded the corner of the house, they saw four guys dumping coolers of ice onto a man who was sprawled out across the bonfire. A putrid yet enticing aroma filled the air; a mixture of burnt liver, seared flesh, and charred meat with metallic overtones. Some of the women had turned aside to vomit, which added insult to injury. The grotesque smell quickly spread over the area. Veronica gasped and hid her face against Bobby's shoulder. A low buzz hissed through the gathering crowd – questions being asked, snippets of conversations that led nowhere, cell phones beeping.

When the ice first made contact with the body, a putrid stench and an angry sizzle hissed into the air. Three of the men that had dumped the coolers were now pulling the body from what was left of the fire. A few sparks jumped across the lawn. The enormous circle of on-lookers backed up in order to give the men room. Meanwhile, Bobby scanned the crowd for G-Force, thinking that he might have seen what happened and had some answers.

Two of the men flipped the body over, face up, while another man cupped his hands around his mouth and yelled.

"Does anyone know who the fuck this guy is?"

Someone from the back of the crowd answered. "Don't you mean *was*?"

"This isn't funny," the first man responded.

The man that was pulled from the fire began screaming. The horrified crowd moved farther back as a single unit, a hive mind, in a feeble attempt to distance themselves from this nightmare. The screams soared into shrieks and then into howls of pain. When the man tried to move his arm, an audible snap and pop echoed throughout the yard like a twig breaking off from a dead tree. His eyes flew open, making the distinction between his blackened charred face and the whites of his eyes more pronounced. He tried to move his left leg, but his jeans were already adhered to his skin. Clothing and tissue ripped with each flinch. His screams continued.

"Call 9-1-1!" Someone yelled from the crowd.

"Can't somebody do something to help him?" another voice called out.

Veronica tugged at Bobby's jacket, still hiding her face among his leather sleeve. "I wanna get out of here. *Now.*"

"Yeah, yeah, we will. Let me see if I can find G. He might want to leave this shit, too."

Bobby and Veronica walked among the throngs of on-lookers who were captivated by the atrocity in front of them. As they passed through the people, they caught bits and pieces of conversations. Some sounded genuinely concerned for the man, while others continued chatting as if they were rudely interrupted by this display of self-destruction.

"Hey, there he is," Bobby said, pointing to a small gathering hovering near a group of garbage cans.

"Say, Bobby, is this some crazy shit or what?"

"Did you see what happened? Me an' Veronica were just over there talking and all of a sudden we heard a gunshot or something. Wouldn't you say that's what it sounded like?" Bobby looked at Veronica for her take on the situation. She nodded, still clinging to Bobby's arm as if her life depended on it.

A man standing next to G-Force answered.

"Yeah, man. We saw the whole thing. This dude starts freaking out, climbs up that lattice work against the house, and takes a fuckin' nose dive off the roof right into the damn fire."

"Why the hell would he *do* something like that?" Bobby asked, eyeing each one of the men in the circle. Not one of them met his gaze. Bobby's question lay dead in the water. They looked at the ground and shrugged their shoulders.

"This is fuckin' bullshit. Let's get out of here, Veronica. G, you want a ride?"

"No, man, I'm good."

As they started to leave, the blaring sirens of emergency vehicles pierced through the night. Bobby looked back. Only a handful of people now stood around the burnt man. Apparently, most of the gawkers had disappeared into the surrounding woods.

CHAPTER 14
THE FINCHON MOTEL

▲ ▲ ▲

"THAT'S RIGHT, SIR. YOU'LL DRIVE down Murphy Road 'til you get to the ol' Citgo Station. Yep. Then take a sharp left and head south for oh, I'd say four miles as the crow flies. You'll see a sign for our place as soon as you cross over into Badfish. Yep, that'll do. Can't miss us. We're the only motel in town. Alrighty then. We'll see you soon. Bye, now."

"Actual customers?" Karl asked as he passed through the office on his way to the stock room. "Huh. Well, you know which room to put them in."

"Room 235. A heck of a steal at fifty-four dollars, if you ask me."

"I wasn't really asking you, Leonard, but thanks for the input. You're going to be here to show them around, right?"

"Planning on it. They're coming in from Knobby Hill, so they ought to be pulling in our parking lot, in, oh, I'd say about twenty minutes. I got it covered, boss."

"Good. I'll be in my office." Karl closed the door on the last syllable. He didn't need any stories from Leonard today.

He had shipments to organize and distribute from his last meeting with Manny.

A gold colored Toyota Camry pulled into the parking lot of the Finchon exactly twenty minutes later. Leonard peeked out from between the blinds and saw that the couple had arrived. He was excited about playing host to actual tourists because that meant he could engage in conversations that didn't revolve around cleaning up vomit or demands for more towels. The best part was that they probably wouldn't reek of urine. Leonard primped in the little mirror on the service desk before greeting the new arrivals.

"Welcome, folks. Glad you made it. How was the trip? Did you have any trouble finding the place? Were the directions helpful?"

"Fine, no and yes," Chaz said, meeting Leonard's extended hand with his own for a gentlemanly shake.

"Uh, umm," Leonard faltered for a moment, forgetting the order of his own questions.

"Everything's fine. We made it, we're here and we're exhausted. It was supposed to be a two and a half hour drive from our house, but we made some unexpected detours. And when you add in lunch, well…four hours later and here we are."

"It's my fault," Lillian said. "There were some tea shops that I just had to go in. I'm what you might call a tea connoisseur, so I'm always on the lookout for new ones to try. But at least we won't have to buy tea for a few months now."

"A few *years*, maybe," Chaz whispered to Leonard. Both men smiled and nodded at each other.

"Well, let me show you to your room and tell you about some of the other amenities you can enjoy during your stay with us. I'll grab some keys and we'll be on our way."

Before they had time to finish unloading the car, Leonard had returned with two sets of keys. He led them to their room, unlocked the door and held it open for the couple to enter first. The scent of ammonia and Lemon Pledge hit them like a brick wall.

"Wow," Lillian said. "That's some cleaner you guys must use."

"Give it a few minutes an' you won't even notice it anymore. And feel free to open a window if you want." He pushed the heavy drapes back and cranked open one of the windows. A foul odor and the sounds of two men cussing wafted through the torn screen. Leonard closed the window. "Or not. It's gets chilly at night around here."

"Actually, after we relax a bit, we probably won't be in the room much at all. Gonna do some hiking near Coral Creek and Sandstone."

"Why, that sounds pretty good. You know, if you're into fishing, they have a place just about twenty, thirty miles from here. I tell ya, though, if you ask me, nothing beats fishing up in the UP. You folks ever heard of the UP? No? That's what they call the Upper Peninsula in Michigan. It's a heck of a place if you're into camping in the great outdoors. Why, I'll bet you two love camping. Yep, I can spot an outdoorsy couple a mile away. Don't tell me now, let me guess. You do all the hunting and your pretty wife here gets to do all the cleaning and prepping, huh? Did I nail it or what? You fish, don't you, Chaz?"

"No, can't say that I do. I've tried it before, but it's not really my thing. I think your crystal ball is a little out of whack there, Leonard. We're not what you'd call the fishing and camping type," he said. Lillian wrinkled her nose and shook her head at the very idea.

"Well, alrighty then," Leonard sighed.

He finished showing them the room and then brought them back into the main office to finish checking in. After exchanging a credit card for a receipt, Chaz and Lillian took a couple of extra bags from the car and went back to their room.

"He's a nice enough guy, didn't you think? Talks a lot, but nice," Chaz said, flipping through the TV channels.

"Yeah, Leonard's a real hometown kind of guy. And you *do* realize this place was a pretty good find for the price. It's not exactly what I'd call fancy, but it'll work for what we need. I told you I could get us a decent motel that wouldn't eat up all our vacation money," Lillian called out from the bathroom, the door slightly ajar.

"You've got to be kidding. Eleven channels and four of them are religious crap?"

"What? I can't hear you, wait a minute."

"Nothing, I was just…"

"What? Hang on; I'll be out in a minute."

"Don't worry. I was just talking to..."

"I can't hear you, hang on."

Her last statement was followed by a very loud toilet flush. "Okay," she stepped over to the sink, "go ahead. What did you say?"

"Nothing really. I was just saying that the TV choices pretty much suck. I can't get anything but the Weather Channel, local news and televised church services. We might have to go into Coral Creek tonight just to have something to do. And we can forget about using the pool. Did you notice how nasty that was?"

"Yeah, it was pretty bad. The website's reviews made it sound so much better than it actually is. Leonard said that they were refurbishing it, but I don't think anyone's even started. I don't know; maybe this won't be all that bad. I mean we're going to be out and about tomorrow and the next day. All we need is a decent place to sleep and take a shower."

"Yeah, I s'pose. It's still light out. Maybe after a short nap we can walk around and check things out in the big town of Badfish."

"And get something to eat," Lillian added.

"Definitely. Hey, were there any pictures of this place on the website?"

"Yeah, a few, but now that I'm seeing it in person, the pictures were pretty misleading. You know, I'll bet the owner got his friends to write good reviews because no one in their right mind would give *this* motel five stars."

Chaz sighed heavily and peered out of a hole in the curtain.

"Yeah, that's for sure. Well, let's try and make the best of it, okay? I'm going to hit the bathroom. Give me a few minutes, huh?"

Lillian smiled and went over to hug Chaz. "Okay. It's all yours. You can borrow my book for reading material if you need."

"No thanks, I'm good." He laughed and hugged her again. When he flipped on the bathroom light, he gasped.

"What is it?" Lillian asked as she rummaged through her suitcase.

"We have a major problem. Get Leonard on the phone and have him come over this second."

▲ ▲ ▲

"I can't imagine how this happened, folks. I'll gladly get a mop and bucket and clean it up right away."

"Leonard, my wife and I aren't exactly troublemakers, but this is really unacceptable. I have never stayed anywhere that had a cesspool flooding out from a toilet being flushed, and that includes a few dumpy motels in Chicago. I mean, look at this. *Needles? Pills?* I'm getting typhoid just looking at this crap."

"I really am sorry, you guys. This is a first for us, I swear," Leonard lied.

He hated to lie, especially to a nice couple that only wanted what any normal guest would want, but he was trying to spare himself from utter embarrassment and the motel from a lawsuit.

"I, uh, I don't think this is going to work out for us, Leonard. Nothing personal, but this is a little too much to overlook. Lillian?"

"Yeah, I agree. I think we're going to need a refund."

When the three of them returned to the main office, Karl was at the service counter. He noticed that the couple was carrying their suitcases and their room keys.

"Checking in?"

"No, boss. They're actually checking out. The toilet overflowed and it was a real mess. These nice folks would like a refund."

"A refund? For a faulty toilet? Did you offer to clean it up for them?"

"It was more than a little water on the floor," Chaz said, stepping up to the counter. He towered over Karl by a good five inches and outweighed him by at least fifty pounds. Karl took half a step back. "The floor was covered in sewage. No, it was actually worse than that. There were needles and bloody strips of gauze and pieces of broken pills and…it was sickening. Actually, from what I saw come out of that toilet, it makes me question what kind of place you're running here."

"Now, you shouldn't make any hasty judgments. We are in the middle of remodeling. Have you seen our pool area? Sure, it's not much to look at now, but in six months you will be begging to book a room with us. Things like that take time. You can't hold us accountable for problems that happened years ago."

"This isn't <u>The Shining,</u> and this place isn't haunted by ghosts from the past; it's filthy and a health hazard. We can overlook the greasy tub, the hair all over the floor, the peeling paint, the obviously thin walls, and the fifteen-watt light bulbs. But the toilet thing was too much. We'd like a refund now, please."

Karl rubbed his face and shifted his footing. This had to be handled very carefully.

"I tell you what. Let me have Leonard show you our *better* room. The rate is a little higher but I will let you have it for the original rate of your first room--fifty-four dollars. Usually for an upgrade like this, we would charge ninety-nine dollars so you are actually getting quite a deal here."

"No. Sorry, but we're done. Do you need to see my credit card in order to run the refund?"

"Please. Let me just show you the room. If you don't like it, then I will give you your money back. Surely that's fair, isn't it?"

Chaz and Lillian exchanged glances. He could tell that she was about to give in, but he stood firm.

"No. I'm not comfortable having my wife stay here."

Karl changed his tactic. "Ma'am, I can see you are wavering. Just a two-minute look at the other room, that's all I'm asking. You have my word that it will be cleaner and larger than the other one. Deal?"

Lillian started to agree; both in her posture and her facial expression, but Chaz intervened. He didn't like Karl and the longer they stayed in the office bickering back and forth, the more he wondered if they would actually get their money back. He realized he should have said something when they first pulled into the parking lot. He had a bad feeling about the place but for Lillian's sake, he wanted to be proved wrong.

"I told you, we're leaving. There is no deal to be had."

"Very well," Karl snapped. Without another word, he shuffled through some papers, angrily punched numbers into a calculator, took Chaz's credit card and returned it with a new receipt.

"There you are. A full refund as you requested."

"Thank you. Lillian, let's go."

"Thanks. Bye." She turned and looked back at Karl and Leonard before walking out the door.

CHAPTER 15

NINA

▲ ▲ ▲

NINA HAD JUST FINISHED A double shift at Bickley's and was exhausted. Some nights were pretty challenging, not that she minded. Extra money always came in handy. But her feet were killing her – damn those high heels – and there were not one but *two* bachelor parties she had to contend with tonight.

Bachelor parties were a necessary evil when working in a strip club. Every dancer inevitably learns their own way of dealing with drunks, loud mouths, handsy grabbers, and the odd troll that sits next to the stage with his tongue hanging out while he rubs on himself. But entertaining for *bachelor parties* usually required the performers to be more vigilant.

During tonight's show, it had felt like everyone in the audience assumed Nina was dancing solely for *him*, which enabled the drunken bastards to yell every foul, dirty, degrading come-on they could think up. A few of the more inebriated ones attempted to climb on the stage and grab at anything they could get their grubby hands on and since Bickley never hired enough bouncers to watch the door *and* the stage at the same time, things got ugly fast.

Nina was right in the middle of her second number when one of the grooms-to-be hoisted himself onto the stage and began tearing off her pirate costume – the one that cost fifty bucks and was a special order from *Struttin' Strippers*. The asshole managed to grab a fistful of pantaloons before one of the other dancers heard the ruckus onstage and ran out from the back. Between the two of them, they were able to shove the guy back down to his table where the rest of his buddies high-fived each other and made whooping noises. By the time Bobby got there, the chaos was over but Nina was pissed.

When the second bachelor party arrived, Nina was already on the defensive and asked Bobby to stay close. Unfortunately, this particular group was far too drunk to enjoy anything. Nina had been collecting decent tips during the first song, but by the second one, three of the guys started puking on the floor. The sight was bad enough but the odor was truly show stopping. Gagging, Nina quickly collected her things from the stage and ran off to the dressing room.

After the frustrating end to a very trying shift, Nina drove back to the Finchon. The only thing on her mind was taking a hot shower and going to bed. She tossed her purse and keys on the little table in the corner and threw her costume into a laundry basket. She went into the bathroom and was about to turn on the shower when she heard a knock at the door.

"Go away," she yelled.

"Miss Dumont?"

"Not interested. Go away."

"Please, Miss Dumont? May I have a minute of your time? It's Karl."

He heard a very audible huff from her side of the door. Once she opened it, she saw Karl holding a bottle of wine, two glasses and a single red rose. She was almost overcome by the scent of Aqua Velva. His velour sweater, tight striped pants and black motorcycle boots screamed 1970s. She covered her mouth to stifle a laugh.

"You're kidding," she managed.

"Miss Dumont? I believe we got off on the wrong foot when you first arrived here and I'd like to make that up to you."

"At one in the morning? Dressed like *that*? Are you serious?"

"Yes, very. Please, all I ask is that you give me five minutes. Then, I'll leave it up to you if you want me to leave. If so, then I will only see you once a month to collect your rent."

Nina faced Karl keeping one hand on the doorknob and the other against the door frame. In the scope of a few seconds, Nina debated on whether to deal with this silly man head on or face the possibility of future impromptu visits from him.

"Five minutes. But if I decide after two minutes that I want you to leave, then you leave. Got it?"

"Of course. You're in charge."

Nina stepped aside and allowed Karl to pass. She glanced outside to see if anyone saw this exchange and then shut the door. When she turned around, Karl was at the small table pouring wine into the glasses he brought. As he set the bottle down, he motioned for her to join him, patting the chair next to his.

"Let me make a toast: to the most beautiful occupant at the Finchon. I should say that I'm honored to have you stay here instead of anywhere else."

"It was the cheapest place, not to mention the only motel in Badfish, so doesn't flatter yourself."

They clinked glasses and drank. Karl drained his glass and refilled it. He offered to pour more for Nina.

"Sure, why not? I sure as hell won't turn down free alcohol. After a night like this, it really hits the spot, you know?"

Karl smiled and raised his glass again.

Perfect.

CHAPTER 16

BICKLEY'S

▲ ▲ ▲

DONALD BICKLEY WAS REVIEWING THE receipts for last month's bar invoices in his office, a task he normally did on *Sunday* nights. But this week, he postponed the task until the following Tuesday in order to coincide with Nina's schedule. He wanted to be there -- to talk to her, to inhale her presence, to see if she had found a safe place to live. If she could only understand how much he wanted her, maybe he would actually have a chance. He looked at the clock on his desk. 8:45pm.

Through his door, he heard Nina and a few of the others chatting and carrying on as they walked down the hall toward the dressing room.

Right on time.

He moved quietly and cracked the door open. He could smell her perfume instantly.

While some of the other dancers were making final adjustments to their costumes, Donald popped his head through the curtain divider.

"Hey, Nina, could you come in my office for a second?"

She whispered something to the other girls that he couldn't make out, but it made them giggle. She followed him back and sat down on the couch.

"Am I in some kind of trouble?"

"You? Of course not. I just haven't had a chance to ask you about how things have been going since our last, um, chat together," Donald said. He didn't want to appear nervous but he felt himself growing hard at the very sight of her.

"Our chat?"

"Sure. You remember. When you told me about getting evicted?"

"Oh, yeah, of course. Geez, I mean, how could I forget somebody giving me that kind of money? Thanks again, Mr. Bickley. I really appreciated it."

"Well?"

"Well what?"

"Did you find a decent place? I've been anxious to hear all about it."

"Well, uh...," Nina grasped for the right words. "Yeah, I found a really great place. It's kind of out in the boonies so I don't think you'd know of it. It's sort of a new apartment complex. I guess it's closer to Clambake than Badfish. Sorry I didn't mention it earlier."

"Huh, I don't remember reading about any new construction going on over there, but then again, I don't get over to that area much. Do you know which company is putting 'em up? Is it Anderson's? I hear they're pretty good."

"I-uh-I don't really know that. I just dealt with the rental office, you know?"

Donald nodded. He scribbled a little note to himself on his desk calendar.

"Do you have the same roommates?"

"Uh, no. Actually, they decided to do their own thing so I just live there by myself. But I don't mind. It's a nice place. Small. Perfect for one, you know? I really should be getting ready...," she gestured toward the door.

"Sure, yeah. I just wanted to hear about your new place. And, uh...I guess I wanted to check to see if you needed any more... assistance."

"Um, not really, everything's good. I guess I can always use extra money, though. But you don't have to..."

"Just think of it as an investment."

"Investment?" she asked and stood up, hand on the doorknob.

"I'm investing in *you*, Nina. You're really special to me. I need you to know that." He walked over, put a sealed envelope into her hands and sat back down at his desk.

"Uh, thanks, Mr. Bickley," she stumbled over something else to say. "I guess I'll see ya later."

He watched her go and then continued to stare blankly at the spot where she last stood before leaving. Donald placed his thumb and forefinger on the crotch of his pants and squeezed himself through the fabric.

Nina strutted onto the stage in full princess regalia, a sparkling crown atop her head. Long flowing drapes of see-through mesh swept close to her feet as she twirled around the center pole. She spun and then tugged at the Velcro patches that held two pieces of the dress together, and suddenly she was a palace slave girl. The costume change received a smattering of applause and hoots from the audience.

Donald had stepped behind the bar and positioned himself directly in front of a keg with a spigot. It was the perfect height for pressing his groin against if he straddled it and bent his knees at the right angle. The combination of watching Nina and pressing against the hardness of the handle was enthralling. Donald thought that her costume change was the best thing he had seen all week.

Nina knew she had his eye, so she got down on all fours and started to crawl and writhe on the floor. She reached behind her back and unhooked what was left of the outfit. She touched herself. Donald stared so intently, his eyes dried from lack of blinking. The more she gyrated on the floor, slapping her ass and massaging her own tits, the harder and faster he thrust his groin into the keg's valve. The moment she arched her back at the climax of the song, Donald's masturbatory execution on the nozzle disconnected the hose from the main pump. The back section of the bar, including Donald, was drenched by a geyser of cheap beer.

CHAPTER 17

VERONICA

▲ ▲ ▲

VERONICA WAS ELBOW DEEP IN toilet water, scrubbing the underside of the seat when the phone rang. She tossed the scrub brush on the floor in disgust but it bounced back into the toilet bowl.

"Shit."

She snapped off her rubber gloves and picked up the phone from the living room table.

"Hello?"

"Hi, Veronica? It's Tracy. Just wanted to see what you're up to. I haven't heard from you in a while an' I was startin' to worry."

"Yes, mom, I'm fine," she chided. "I'm only like, what, four months younger than you?"

"Five."

"Okay, five, four, ten. I don't care. What's up?"

"I wanted to hear about the big date. You haven't told me anything yet."

"Oh," Veronica giggled a little. "With Bobby, you mean. Yeah, he's pretty nice. I think you'd like him."

"Come on! Don't keep me in suspense. How was it? Did he actually take you to the Sea Grass in Coral Creek?"

"Yes, and it was amazing. I have never been to a place like that in my whole life. They actually had waiters just standing around waiting to fill your water glass."

"Oh, my God. I hear its crazy expensive, too. Nothing like that in Badfish."

"I know. I couldn't believe it when he said we were going there. I was like, no, really, where are we going? Tracy, I swear, I didn't think I had clothes good enough to wear to this place."

"So, how was the food? Incredible?"

"Pretty much. I didn't even recognize half the stuff they brought. I mean, they explained it when they put the dishes in front of us, but I couldn't tell you what they were talking about."

"Yeah, really," Tracy added.

"When the bill came, he was in the bathroom."

"You didn't!"

"Yes, I did! I snuck a look at it."

"Well?"

"You ready for this? For two people, the bill was $150. And that's before a tip. Can you believe it?"

"Jesus. That's like half of my paycheck. Did he say anything when he saw how much it was?"

"Nope. He just opened it up, looked at the amount and took out his wallet."

"Oh, my gosh."

"You know what's kind of weird though? He asked if I wanted to go there again."

"Why is that weird? It sounds great to me."

"Because I know where he works, Tracy. There's no way he's making that kind of money at Bickley's, you know what I mean?"

"Yeah, I guess. So where do you think he's getting that kind of money? You think he has another job?"

"*In this town?* No, I think I'd know about it if that were the case."

"Maybe he won the lottery."

"He's living at the Finchon. No one in their right mind would live there if they won a bunch of money. I don't know. Maybe he's been socking it away 'cause he's sure not spending it on rent."

There was a pause in the conversation.

"Well...you could always just ask him, Veronica."

"I don't think that would go over too well. We just started going out; it's not really my business. For all I know, his parents are sending him money. But I guess as long as he's willing to take me back there, *what difference does it make?*"

Tracy sensed that Veronica was a bit miffed by her question. She did have a point. *Who were they to question where a guy got his money?* The only thing Bobby Price was guilty of was trying to show Veronica a good time. Was there truly anything wrong with that?

"You're right. Sorry."

"It's okay. Before you know it, all three of us are going to be getting the hell out of Badfish. We'll have awesome jobs and be able to eat at places like The Sea Grass every week."

"The sooner the better. I can't wait to get the heck out of this place, once and for all."

CHAPTER 18

ROOM 205

▲ ▲ ▲

A CACOPHONY OF SOUNDS WOKE the tenants on either side of Room 205 at a few minutes past one a.m. It would be a bleary start to a Tuesday since most of the motel's residents had been fast asleep for less than an hour. Disturbances like this were fairly common on the weekends, but for the few people that worked during the week, even if it was just the occasional odd job, a decent night's sleep was vehemently protected.

The sounds from Room 205 started out as muffled moans. Soon after, they morphed into a steady cry and now had ramped up to a full-fledged wail. Bangs and thumps came next; it sounded like furniture was being thrown against the walls and ceiling. At this point, a few occupants from the neighboring rooms opened their doors and peered out. After an initial nod of acknowledgement to each other, they gathered in front of the room in question, shrugging their shoulders, putting ears against the door, and shaking their heads. Curiosity hadn't quite turned into concern yet.

"What's going on in there, man?"

"I dunno. Who's in there?"

"New guy. Moved in about a week ago. I only seen him once or twice."

"Hey," a woman tenant joined in. "What the hell is going on in there? Did someone knock?"

"Knock? You think they're going to hear us knocking over all that shit?"

"Well, somebody needs to do something. People gotta work in the morning, you know."

A few others joined the small group, asking questions but not volunteering to take any kind of action. The commotion suddenly stopped, ending with what sounded like a balloon pop. Everyone looked at each other and held a moment of silence.

"Shit," the woman said. "Someone's gotta go in there and find out what happened."

"Fuck that," a voice from the back of the group said. "I'm not cleaning up after some druggie's bad trip."

"Well, I'm not gonna stand here while someone bleeds out," the woman countered. She pounded on the door and yelled toward the door jamb. "Hey! Hey you inside 205! My name's Shondra. Can you let me in?"

"How the fuck you gonna help? What are you, a nurse or something?"

"No, I'm not a fuckin' nurse, but I'm not gonna just stand around like you assclowns and do nothing if somebody needs help."

She continued yelling and pounding on the door as more neighbors gathered around. A few others joined in the pounding against the door and window, trying to get the occupant of 205 to answer. A large man from the first floor stepped in front of Shondra.

"Here, look out. I'm gonna kick the door in."

By this time, a healthy sized crowd had gathered around the front of the doorway, Bobby Price among them. Someone from the back of the group yelled. "You can't kick down the door. The owner will kill ya."

"Not before he sends him a bill for it," another man added. Spurts of laughter rippled through the crowd.

"Fuck all that," the kicking man muttered. He took a few steps back and hurled his entire body into the door.

"I thought he was gonna kick it," someone said. The statement was met with a few chuckles.

The door and adjoining walls creaked as if they were partially broken inside. The first attempt wasn't enough, so the man stepped back again, took a deep breath and threw his body against the door as hard as he could. The second time did the trick. The busted door flew open, exposing Room 205 and all of its contents to over a dozen sets of eyes.

"Holy shit," someone gasped.

Shondra pushed her way inside before anyone else, shaking her head in disbelief.

"Looks like a damn tornado went through here."

With a great deal of hesitation, the group of on-lookers made their way into the room. They whispered quietly among themselves, trying to take in what they were seeing and being very careful not to touch anything. All four walls were covered in what appeared to be a mosaic pattern. All the furniture had been toppled over, including the twin bed. The mattress was leaning off to one side with an assortment of clothes draped over it, all of which were covered with the same pattern. The only area that didn't feature the artistic element was the carpet; it had dark track marks all over it and smelled burnt.

Shondra called out from the bathroom. "No one in here. I don't know where the hell he could have gone. I mean, we were all outside the door an' as far as I know, there's no other way out of here."

Bobby Price spoke up, pointing at something and trying not to gag. "That...that...is..."

"What, man?" someone standing next to the mattress asked.

"That...is the guy. He's on the wall."

Every person in the room moved closer to an area of wall to inspect what they had initially believed was an intricate paint job. Most rooms at the Finchon had chipping paint, peeling borders, and in some extreme cases, crumbling drywall. It didn't dawn on anyone that the interior design of this room was different than their own until Shondra screamed.

"He's right. There's a fingernail over here." She cupped her hand over her mouth in wide-eyed horror.

"I think I'm looking at part of a toe," the large man who busted down the door groaned.

"Fuck all that, I think I found a piece of his dick," somebody else choked out. "What the hell?"

Collectively, the group took a step back toward the middle of the room. The ghastliness of what surrounded them hadn't completely sunk in: the pieces on the walls, the bloody drips from the ceiling, the burns on the carpeting, the odor of sizzled flesh. Bobby put it together first and said it out loud. His statement forced the surrealistic scene into reality.

"*This guy* was the tornado. See the lines on the carpet and how they cross over each other and go around the room? He was probably spinning out of control. I bet that's why all the furniture and stuff is knocked over."

"What's that have to do with all the shit on the walls?"

"It's *him*, man, don't you see? The body parts?"

"*Spun into pieces?* Is that what you're saying?" Shondra asked.

Bobby could tell she hated saying it. The words left a sick residue in her mouth and hung in the air like strips of used fly paper.

"That's bullshit. Nothin' like that really happens. You two must be readin' some sci-fi shit or something."

"Well, what do *you* think happened?" Bobby said, folding his arms across his body. "From everything that I see, yeah, that's exactly what it looks like to me. If you have a better explanation, I'd like to hear it."

"Come on, yo," the sci-fi proposing man said. "Let's get outta here. This place smells like fuck-all anyway."

One by one, the crowd dispersed. They filed out of Room 205, walked down the hallways and disappeared into their own rooms. Bobby and Shondra remained, standing in the doorway, trying to make sense of the scenario.

"Do you really think that's what happened to him? That he spun outta control 'til he just broke apart?"

"To be honest, I really don't want to think about that happening to someone...but, yeah. It sure looks that way to me. How else could you explain what's in that room? Did you *know* this guy?"

"No," Shondra admitted. "But I kinda wish I did now. Maybe if I did, I could've stopped this, you know? God, living here really sucks – there's so much garbage that goes on. There are so many people that are...troubled."

Bobby nodded.

"Do you think we should call the manager or go down to the office and tell them? I'd hate to just walk away and not do anything."

"I'll take care of it," Bobby assured her. "Don't worry, okay? Go on back to your room. You don't want to get involved in this stuff."

"Well, what about you? You shouldn't get involved in something like this either."

"That's okay. I'll be fine. Please, just...just go on. I'll make sure the manager knows about it, alright?"

She hesitated for a moment. "Well, I suppose. My name's Shondra, by the way. I'm in 217, down that way." She pointed down the dark hallway.

"I'm in 303. Bobby Price."

"Shondra Cullen," she extended her hand. "Nice to meet you."

"You, too. Thanks." He awkwardly shook her hand and smiled.

"For what? I didn't do anything except look around some guy's fucked up room."

"You *stayed*. That's something."

"Alright, Bobby Price in Room 303. Be careful, okay?"

"I will. Promise." Bobby gave a little wave as he watched Shondra walk down the hall to her room.

He placed the hinge-less door up against the doorframe of 205, creating a makeshift barricade with him on the inside. The useless lock hung listlessly on the wall but he latched it to what was left of the bolt on the door. It was an attempt to have some privacy. Bobby gingerly walked through the man's room, gazing at the splattered walls, sickened and fascinated by the traces of black on the carpet. He entered the bathroom, which by comparison to the main room, was a major improvement. He opened the drawers in the vanity and looked in the medicine cabinet.

Finally, out of the corner of his eye, he saw it. Behind the dirty toilet, almost completely obscured by wads of Kleenex and toilet paper, lay a syringe. Bobby took a towel from the counter and wrapped it around his hand. Slowly, he bent down, scooted aside the garbage and moved the syringe closer in order to get a better look. He kneeled on the tile floor, eyeing it methodically. The plunger had been pushed about halfway down, leaving the vial's body partially full of a bright orange liquid. The needle was still attached; orange contents seeped out in a thin stream.

"Fuck."

Bobby removed the towel from his hand and threw it into the tub. He sat down cross legged on the floor directly in front of the syringe and touched it. It was warm. He caressed it lovingly and closed his eyes. He lay down in front of it and placed his nose right up against the point of the needle. A tiny drop of the orange drug bubbled onto his skin. He giggled and pushed his nose further forward. A miniscule drop of blood oozed from a single pore where contact with the needle had been made.

He rubbed his nose; it smeared the two liquids together, leaving a tiny smudge. Bobby sat up and took the syringe in his right hand. He pointed the needle into his mouth. With his tongue out, he laid the point down to face the back of his throat. All he had to do was push the plunger the rest of the way and he would be filled with a powerful rush that he'd never felt before. A single press on a plastic plunger...

CHAPTER 19

DATE NIGHT

▲ ▲ ▲

"NINA, YOU LOOK AMAZING."

Karl stood just inside the doorway to her room, eyes caressing her from head to toe and back again.

"Thanks, Karl," she purred. "You look pretty good yourself tonight."

He smiled, shut the door behind him and moved toward the bed.

"So, tell me. What do you have planned for our first official date? Let me guess - dinner and a movie? Or maybe pizza at your place? Or better yet - sex in your hot tub?"

"How about one of each?" he smirked, leaning back against the pillows, hands folded on his stomach.

"Uh huh. I kind of figured you were just out for some free pussy."

"*Nothing's* free, dear. Everything has a price. You just have to figure out what it is and which people are willing to sell. And no, I'm *not* just after that, because if that's all I was looking for, I'd simply hang out at Bickley's at closing time."

"You *do* know I work there, don't you? Those girls you're talking about are my friends."

"Come on…it's the nature of the business. I get the fact that you dance for money. Most of the time, that's the only reason anyone would do something like that. But you can't seriously tell me that there isn't one single girl that works there that's *not* willing to do other stuff for extra cash under the table, so to speak."

"How am I supposed to know what every single person does on their off time? I just know that I don't, and I'm a little pissed off that you think I would. Maybe this date wasn't such a good idea after all. I mean, I'm not some whore you can just fuck anytime you want just 'cause I live *here* and work *there*."

"Hold on a minute," Karl started to back pedal. "I didn't mean to offend you, that wasn't my intention. I was only saying that some people working at Bickley's might have, uh, different motivations than yourself, that's all."

"And what if they do? So what?"

"Just that *like* company tends to hang around *like* company."

"What's that supposed to mean? That I'm easy just 'cause other girls that work there might be?"

Karl sat up and cleared his throat. He didn't like where the conversation or its implications were going. If she ended up too angry, he'd never get any tonight.

"Look. I'm sorry. Let's start over. Why don't we just go out and have a nice evening, okay? Nina, you look absolutely amazing tonight."

She forced a smile. Karl's own motives were sounding a little questionable to her, but she knew that being a stripper came with certain connotations and pre-conceived notions automatically attached to it. It also wasn't the first time that a man broached the subject of trading sex for money. And as long as she worked at Bickley's or any other strip joint, it probably wouldn't be the last.

Money *was* the main reason she took the job in the first place. Now, with Donald Bickley showering her with cash anytime she asked for it, why leave and give that up? The extra she made while dancing was just icing on the cake.

If it turned out that Karl Demetris was interested in her as well, she could end up with quite a financial windfall. Having the two wealthiest men in Badfish each vying for her attention, each willing and able to laud her with gifts and fancy dinners, could end up being quite lucrative for her in the long run.

She thought about it for a moment. Why argue with Karl about ethical and moral differences between being a stripper and being a hooker when there was money to be made? Debating over semantics with a sleazy businessman would just be a waste of precious time.

"Why, thank you, Karl. And might I say that you look pretty hot yourself," she said. "I'm ready to go."

"Perfect," he said, holding out his elbow for her to take. "I might even have a few tricks up my sleeve."

They shared a fake laugh. Nina took Karl's elbow as they exited the dump of a motel room and walked over to his red Aston-Martin in the parking lot across from the main office.

▲ ▲ ▲

Two hours, a light supper and four drinks later, Nina stumbled back up the stairs to her room with Karl right behind her. His hands were placed directly on each ass cheek, squeezing them slightly with every step she took. She giggled and hiccupped and fished in her purse for her keys in front of her door.

"They're in some, herewhere...wait...um...," she muttered.

"I think someone had a bit too much to drink tonight. Why don't you let me do that for you," Karl offered as he reached for her purse and pulled out a set of keys off the top. He opened the door and escorted her inside. "How about if you change into something more comfortable while I get us something to drink? Something non-alcoholic, that is."

"M'okay...I'll be right here," she slurred, falling onto the bed. "Ooof."

She curled up on the bed, one high-heeled shoe dangling off of her toes, and instantly started to snore. Karl waited, making certain that Nina was out of commission before tip toeing out the door. He headed to the office where Neil was gently resting his head on his arms on the service counter. Karl picked up a stack of Neil's comics and dropped them next to the boy's head.

"Wha?"

"I'm not paying you to nap, Neil. Wake up."

"Sorry, Mr. D," Neil yawned and stretched. "Kinda slow tonight, you know?"

"Maybe for you, kid."

Karl grabbed two cold water bottles from his personal refrigerator in his office and walked around to face Neil.

"Try staying awake this time, huh?"

"Got it, Mr. D. Sorry 'bout that."

Karl raised his chin in acknowledgement and headed back to Nina's room. He stood outside her door and opened one of the bottles. He reached into his coat pocket, pulled out a tiny plastic package containing a fluorescent orange powder and carefully added a few crystal flakes to the open bottle. He screwed the lid back on, shook it for about a minute and tucked the empty plastic package back into his coat.

"Knock, knock, anyone home?" Karl said as he turned the door knob and walked in on a sound asleep Nina.

"Oh, you poor thing. Look at you, sleeping already when there's so much of the evening left. Well, I'll bet all those drinks at dinner made you tired. Probably dehydrated too. The best thing to do in a situation like this is to drink some water."

He sat down on the bed next to Nina and hoisted her up into a seated position. "Come on now, wake up. I brought you something to drink."

"Hnnng," she mumbled as she folded over herself like two-week old flowers.

"There you go. Sit up here next to me," he pressed, trying to keep her in an upright position.

"Wha…wha's gnnn on?"

"You asked me to get you some water, don't you remember? Here, I brought you a brand new bottle. I got one for myself too, so you won't have to drink alone."

"Drnkin'?"

"That's right, drinking. I'll drink mine and you drink yours."

Karl guided the water bottle up to Nina's lips and helped her hold the bottle to her mouth. It was sloppy and messy and some of the liquid ended up on her dress and in her lap, but she did manage to ingest some of it. She wiped her face with her floppy, flailing arm and fell back on to the bed.

"Wonderful." Karl smiled and took a swig from his own bottle.

He capped it, set it down on the floor and carefully positioned Nina on the bed. He pulled the blanket over her and tucked the top edge around her shoulders. He took her empty bottle and threw it in the garbage right before heading to the door. He paused for a moment. Rethinking his last move, he snatched up the empty water bottle, hid it under his coat and turned off the lights.

"G'night, Nina. I'm sure we'll do this again very soon," he whispered into the darkness.

CHAPTER 20

KARL AND LEONARD

▲ ▲ ▲

"HOLY SHIT. WE'RE AT FULL capacity now, Leonard. Except for the rooms set aside for real customers, we're maxed out. Is that fuckin' great or what?"

"Wow. That great news, boss. You must have rented the last few rooms over the weekend, huh?"

"Yes, I did. I told you we needed to fill up and dammit if I didn't make that happen."

"Well, uh, at the rate we keep losing folks, those rooms are gonna empty out faster than we can fill 'em. And, I gotta tell ya, that last room I cleaned was pretty bad. Heck, worst I've seen in quite some time. You ever figure out what all that stuff was on the walls and ceiling? I had to call the carpet cleaners three times before they got those stains out. Actually, if you look real close, you can still make out some of those black lines, but I didn't have the heart to call 'em again. Think maybe we should bite the bullet and replace the carpeting?"

"Hell, no. I'm not spending another dime. Between your overtime and the cleaning crews, that one damn room cost me almost $250. *One fuckin' room, Leonard.* That's not how I want to spend my money. You think I'm going to drop hard earned cash on those bums living up there? Shit. They'd as soon piss all over new carpeting or new bedding or whatever the hell we'd do. It's not worth it. *They're* not worth it."

Leonard started to speak but hesitated. He stood up from the customer service counter and walked into Karl's office. He felt uncomfortable carrying on that kind of conversation across a threshold. It felt too important, more important than their usual banter.

"Karl, can I be frank with you? Now, I know this is your business and far be it from me to tell you how to run it. Heck, I'm just an' ol' farm boy from a little town called Badfish. Why, I couldn't tell you the difference between one accounting sheet from another. But I can tell you this — I remember when the Finchon was *the* place to stay at. Folks would make an effort to drive here just so they could book a room an' swim in the pool an' take a nice, leisurely walk around town. This was a fantastic place at one time, Karl. You've seen photos and I know you've heard some of the stories. You could make it great again. But in order for that to happen, you gotta put some money behind it. Clean it up, in more ways than one if you catch my drift. You could be the one to turn it around. And I tell you what. If you do, why, I'll help you any way I can."

Karl listened to Leonard as he spoke. He held his gaze for a few beats after Leonard was finished and then straightened a paper pile on his desk.

"Thank you for that."

"For what, boss?"

"For that nostalgic trip down memory lane. I appreciate it, I really do. But, Leonard, I'm going to let you in on a little secret."

Leonard sat down in the chair across from Karl; the large mahogany desk stood between them.

"Leonard, you're what now, seventy-three?"

"Sixty-eight."

"Sixty-eight, okay, and you remember how things used to be around here, right? How this was some big shot motel in its day and everyone who had a swagger and a wad of cash would stay here having parties all day and night, correct?"

Leonard nodded.

"And then all of a sudden, the whole place took some kind of fucked up nose dive. And bam! The Finchon goes from having this incredible reputation to becoming some sort of freak show that no one wants to drive by, let alone stay at, right?"

Leonard nodded again.

"Do you think that *I* made all that happen? That everything was perfect and then the minute I bought it, the place goes to hell? Because let me tell *you,* that is not how it happened. This place was on its way down long before I came along. When I took it over, I would have had to put so much money into it to get it back to its original state that I would have been better off building a brand new motel. Yep, maybe I should have leveled this place to the ground and started over from scratch."

"I can understand all that, Karl. But why *didn't* you?"

"Because it wouldn't have been profitable. That's the big difference between you and me. I bought it for the sole purpose of making money, not to be in the hospitality industry. It's not an investment, *it's a write-off.* It's a bad business decision that I can deduct from my taxes each and every year. So, every dollar that I am forced to spend on this piece of crap, for whatever the reason, cuts into my profits. Surely, even *you* can see that."

"What about all the people that live here? Don't they deserve a decent place to stay even if it is just a motel room?"

"This isn't the Salvation Army, Leonard, and I'm not running a homeless shelter. For all practical purposes, this is a business, albeit a bad one, and I'm treating it as such. And since it's actually a motel, what I really should be doing is charging these derelicts by the night, but I'm giving them a break. What other motel would let losers like these hang around, scaring away real customers while they shoot shit into their veins? Or the ones who sit around drunk or hung over in the parking lot? They got it pretty good and they know it. Why do you think most of 'em stick around for so long?"

"But what about people like Eldon?"

"Eldon? Fuck him. You'll always see someone like that completely fuck themselves up over drugs. In his case, he just couldn't handle it. He must have taken too much or mixed it wrong – I don't know. But we took care of it, didn't we? Just like all the others. I know how to handle crises. Clean it up, say nothing and go on about your business."

"Yeah, about that...," Leonard said. His brow furrowed with concern.

"About what?"

"Eldon."

"What *about* Eldon? As far as I'm concerned, that's just old history."

"Well, I never did get a chance to tell you, and I have to say that I'm not completely sure about this, but after I cleaned everything up and loaded him into the pickup truck, I think somebody might have seen me drive away."

"So? You were driving the truck. You've done that plenty of times. There's nothing suspicious about that even if someone did see you."

"Yeah, but I don't know. I'm just getting a bad feeling about *all* this stuff, boss. For some reason I can't quite put my finger on, it just feels like this whole thing is spiraling out of control."

"Leonard, I think you worry too much. Maybe you should take one of your fishing trips this weekend. You know, take a break and relax. As long as you don't say anything to anyone, I don't think we're going to have a problem. You understand, don't you?"

"Of course I do, Karl. I've never said a word to anyone about what goes on here, including the wife. I'm just worried, I guess."

"You leave the worrying to me. That's why *I'm* the businessman and you're *not*."

CHAPTER 21

BICKLEY

▲ ▲ ▲

DONALD BICKLEY WAS ENJOYING A peaceful Sunday at home, reclining in his La-Z-Boy, feet up, remote control in his hand. Minutes earlier, he had polished off a Subway foot-long and two bags of Bar-B-Q chips and was feeling just this side of full. The phone rang, startling him up and out of his longitudinal position. He took a huge swig of Coke before he answered his cell.

"H'llo?"

"Mr. Bickley? This is Nina."

"Nina?" He cleared his throat and took another drink. "Nina. Well, this is unexpected. What can you do for me? I, uh, I mean, what can I do for you?"

"Are you going to be home? I need to come over and talk to you about something."

"Sure. I'll be home all day. Come on by any time you like. You have my address, don't you?"

"Seven fifty eight Moreland, just past the Subway."

"Yes, that's right. I'll see you soon then."

"Bye."

The reality of the situation didn't hit him for a few minutes, but once his brain and his genitals caught up with each other, there was no stopping his thought process. *She's coming here to see me in my house on her day off. She wants me. She wants to fuck me. Not at the club like some other job, but here, right in my own home. There's no other reason she could possibly want to come over on a Sunday. What should I wear? Maybe nothing? No, that's too forward. I wonder if she'll be wearing that short red dress with the black lace stockings and her hair pulled back and those CFM boots. Do I have a drink for her? Shit, I finished the beer last night. I'm hard already. I hope she won't notice right away.*

Donald hadn't realized it but he had been pulling on his ears ever since he hung up. A small oval of wetness began to seep through his sweatpants. He got up and went into his bedroom to change into his terry cloth robe and slippers. The last thing he wanted was for her to think that he *wasn't* interested. He knew the rumors that floated through the town. Fuckin' Karl Demetris did his share to keep them going, the son-of-a-bitch.

He went into the bathroom to tidy up. Shaving cream, bits of dried soap and wayward hairs covered the sink and the counter. He righted towels that were hung askew and picked up rogue squares of toilet paper from the corners of the room. He capped the toothpaste and wiped down the mirror. *Well, if I missed anything else, she'll have to understand the life of a bachelor. I suppose when she starts coming over here on a regular basis, I'll have to stay on the ball to keep this place looking decent. Maybe I'll get some matching towels and some of that smelly stuff that women like. And the toilet seat. I've got to remember to put it down after I piss now.*

Nina didn't mention an arrival time, but Donald wasn't going to be caught off-guard. He needed to make sure that everything was in its place. He wanted her to walk in and see a well kept home, a place that she could feel comfortable in, especially for sleeping over. And once she became familiar with his quirks, she would most certainly be willing to compromise where needed. He imagined that after a few months, Nina would have learned to cook his favorites: meatloaf without onions and well done pot roast, still moist enough to cut into like butter. And pie. Lots of pie.

While he straightened up the kitchen, he pictured Nina bent over in a French maid's outfit, putting a rhubarb pie in the oven and removing the peach one. He'd wait until she was clear of the hot oven to fondle her; his hands caressing her skin as he moved up her short skirt and right down her panties.

He cleaned the living room last. As he fluffed the couch pillows and picked up three days' worth of scattered newspapers and mail, he imagined her lounging on the sofa, glass of wine in one hand and her left titty in the other. She'd always be ready for him. She was years younger so it made perfect sense. Why else would she dress the way she does, provoking those urges in him, taunting him with her sexuality from the stage? She was practically begging him to ravage her right there in front of a roomful of pathetic trolls with constant hard-ons.

He would do it too. If she was willing, he would rip his own clothes off and climb on top of her right in front of those fuckin' animals and God and everybody. It wouldn't be the first time he had screwed in front of other people. But now, it didn't have to go *that* far. She was coming over and they had the whole house to themselves. They could christen every room in their own way and in their own time - no audience needed.

It was going to be wonderful. She could move in as soon as her new lease was up. Hell, he'd pay extra in order for her to break her apartment contract. He'd hire a moving company so she wouldn't have to lift a finger. She could stand in the middle of his living room and point here and there, directing people as to where her things should go. Then, after everyone left and it was just the two of them, he would take her up to his bed and teach her a thing or two about what it meant to belong to Donald Bickley. And she would love it.

He finished fluffing the last pillow on the lounger just as the doorbell rang. It was followed by a soft knock. Donald neatened his hair in the entryway mirror and opened the door.

"Nina, come in. This is such a nice surprise. I can't even remember the last time you were at my house."

"Uh, I was never at your house, Mr. Bickley."

"Well, welcome all the same. Here, let me take your jacket. Make yourself at home. Can I get you something to drink? Sorry I don't have any beer to offer you, but I haven't made it to the store yet. I do have some sodas, though. Or water? I can get you a glass of ice."

"No, um, I'm good. I just wanted to…"

"Something to eat then? I have to apologize; my manners are for shit. That's the bachelor life, huh? What can I make you?

I'll be glad to whip up whatever you want. Ten minutes, I can have it ready."

"No, Mr. Bickley, please. I've *had* lunch. I just needed to talk to you."

"Sure," he said, sitting on the couch next to her, a six inch gap between them. He intended to close the distance before long. "If this is about money, you know all you have to do is ask."

"It's not exactly about money. I've just been -" Nina started, but he cut her off again.

"Is someone bothering you at the club? You're right to come to me if some asshole starts fuckin' with you. I'll kick that son-of-a-bitch right to the curb and not look back. Who is it? That faggy looking one with the blonde hair or that fat piece of shit that wears denim all the time?"

"No, please. Mr. Bickley. Let me explain."

"You're right, I'm sorry. I get a little defensive when it comes to you, Nina. I'm just trying to look out for you. You can understand that, can't you?"

"I wanted to tell you that I haven't been feeling well lately. I need some time off," Nina blurted out. "I don't know if it's the flu or what, but I needed you to know before you started on next week's schedule. I would've come in tomorrow and talked to you, but all I really want to do is go home and get in bed. An' I don't know how long I'll be out. I can call you when I start feeling better. I guess I could have called you now, but... I don't know. I just wanted you to see that I'm not makin' this up."

Donald froze; his mouth agape.

All she wants is time off? No secret love affair? No burning desire to touch me? Not even a grilled cheese sandwich and a warm Coke? What kind of fucked up game is she playing? She asks me for money, which I gladly give her, and this is how she returns the favor? By asking for time off from the club? She's supposed to love me and want to fuck me every single day. She stands up there on the stage, naked, glistening, longing for me. I've seen it. What the hell is happening here?

"Mr. Bickley? Did you hear me?"

He didn't move. He was almost afraid to. What if he blinked and she wasn't even there? Maybe she never even called and wasn't really sitting next to him this very moment. Maybe this was all in his head like a dream, and if he moved from this position, everything about her would vanish into thin air.

"Um, okay…I think I should go now. If I do have the flu, I wouldn't want you to catch anything. I've heard that it's worse for little kids and old people if they get it."

Was she even talking to him? Was the voice he heard really Nina Dumont or was this vision similar to the one in Charles Dickens' A Christmas Carol, one that he could chalk up to eating a bad piece of fish? Might he wake up an hour from now and be visited by the Stripper of Christmas Past? In the morning hours, would he throw open his window and call to some kid passing underneath, asking them to buy the fattest goose in the meat department down at Shopper's Value? Would he wish everyone to have a merry fuckin' Monday?

And did she just call him *old*?

Nina stood up; the bottom of her skirt rested exactly level with Donald's nose. The ruffles brushed against his skin. "I'll call you as soon as I start feeling better, okay?"

She kept her eye on him as she picked up her jacket and walked out the front door.

Donald remained still as his mind continued to race. *What just happened? She was supposed to move in with me. We were going to make plans for the future together. We should have been on my bed right this second, our naked bodies rubbing against each other in a crazy sexual frenzy.*

"Nina?"

CHAPTER 22
BOBBY PRICE

▲ ▲ ▲

BOBBY NEVER THOUGHT THAT IN a million years he would have a problem as fantastic as the one he had now. Twenty-two years old and dating not one girl, but *two,* at the same time no less. It should have been sheer paradise, but in reality it had turned out to be more complicated than he imagined.

Veronica was great. She was hot and sexy and they had a lot of fun. Working together at Bickley's allowed them to talk shop, comparing notes about some of the crazies they encountered during their shifts. She never questioned where he got his extra money and she certainly never complained when he spent it on her. But as the weeks passed, she was becoming more needy and clingy. Bobby didn't particularly care for that nugget of her personality. What was cute at first had quickly become annoying and burdensome.

Shondra was different. From the outset, she carried herself with more confidence. She had an air of independence and understanding. During their times together, he grew to appreciate her insightfulness and regard for others. She was attractive too - not as flashy as Veronica, but pretty in her own way.

Even though there was no real reason that he couldn't continue to see them both, he realized that they would find out about each other at some point. Badfish was too small a town to keep situations like this under wraps. It was like waiting for the proverbial shoe to drop. Anyway, seeing two women was getting expensive. Bobby was making good money selling drugs with G-Force, but that could dry up at any time. Dabbling in illegal business had bad karma written all over it.

In order to address his relationship quandary, Bobby decided to ask each one how they felt about taking things to the next level. That way, he wouldn't have to be the one to make a decision; whoever wanted more of a commitment would be the one he would continue to see. He couldn't see anything wrong with such a solid plan.

Since she lived close, he began with Shondra. He knocked on her door, hoping she was home. He was happy when he saw the curtain move and heard the lock being turned.

"Hey there, Bobby. Come on in."

"Hi, Shondra," he said as he bent over to kiss her. "How are you doing? Not working today, huh?"

"Nope. Got the day off. I switched with Hurley so I could have two days in a row to myself."

"Man, I still don't get how you can work in a nursing home. Isn't that like the most depressing place in the world?"

"Naw, it's not so bad. Some of those folks don't have anybody else 'cept for us workers. It's kind of like having a bunch of grandparents around. Only difference is, you just gotta clean up after them."

"I don't think I could do it. I mean, you actually have to wipe their butt? Like after they shit? Adult diapers and all that?"

"Sometimes, but it's just a part of the job. It's not like they can help it or anything," Shonda said. She put her hands on her hips and continued. "Bobby Price, don't tell me you came all the way over to my room to ask me about old people's poop habits?" she laughed. "Or maybe you're finally thinking of getting into the C.N.A. business instead of the titty business. It would be a nice change for you, I think."

"You do, do you?" Bobby raised an eyebrow. "Well, I can't say at this point that I'm lookin' to make a career change, but I'll keep it in mind."

They laughed. He felt so comfortable talking to her, like they had known each other for years instead of months.

"No, uh, the real reason I came over was to ask you something, but now I'm not really sure how to say it."

Shondra sat down on the bed and folded her legs underneath her. Her face took on a worried expression.

"Oh, oh. Whenever someone starts a conversation like that, usually the rest of it isn't gonna be much better."

"No, no, no," Bobby quickly retorted. "It's nothing like that. Shit, see, I don't know how to do this very well."

Shondra took a deep breath in, held it for a second and then exhaled just as hard. "Go ahead. Say what you gotta say, Bobby Price."

"I, uh, I wanted to know if you wanted us to be exclusive. You know, not see anyone else. Just each other." He pulled at a blanket thread, avoiding her gaze.

"Oh. Oh, Bobby. That's a relief. I thought you really had some bad news to tell me. Oh, geez. That's so sweet of you."

He grinned, but kept looking down, pulling on the thread. "What'cha think?"

"Well, I gotta be honest with you. I'm trying to save up money for school and get my RN degree. I've been thinking about it for a while now. I'm getting sick of living here and barely making ends meet. If I get my nursing degree, things can be a lot different for me. Last week, I went over to the community college in Coral Creek and they told me that if I can pay for the first semester, they might be able to help me get a scholarship for the rest of my schooling. The whole thing would take about a year and a half."

"That's really great, Shondra. Why didn't you tell me last week?"

"Well…I didn't want to say anything until I was sure I was really going to do it. You know, try to set it up and then have it *not* work out."

"Yeah, I get that. When are you supposed to start? I mean, its November already."

"I'd be starting the nursing classes next fall, but first I'd have to take a core biology class. That's what I'm hoping to do in January. And that's the real reason why I switched with Hurley. I'm taking two of her shifts at the nursing home next week. Since it's over Thanksgiving, I'm gonna make double time."

"Wow, Shondra. I don't know what to say. So, you're going to be working *and* going to school at the same time?"

Shondra nodded slowly and took his chin in her hand, raising it slightly. "That's right, Bobby Price. I'm gonna be busy like nobody's business. So, uh, I'd love to keep seeing you and all, but I can't get tangled up in a big relationship right now. I really, really like you but I hope you understand."

"Yeah, of course," he said, looking directly into her eyes and meeting her smile with his. "That's an awesome plan. I'm really happy for you. You definitely *should* focus on that. I just thought I'd ask about us, is all."

"I'm glad you did. And I hope that we can still go out once in a while, 'cause I'm gonna need some study breaks."

"Yeah, yeah, we can do that. We can absolutely do that."

▲ ▲ ▲

With a feeling of accomplishment, Bobby Price drove over to Veronica's apartment. He was singing along to the radio, tapping on the steering wheel, smiling to himself. *Yep, this was going to work out perfectly.* A light snow began sprinkling over the town, yet the temperature remained warm enough to keep the precipitation from sticking to the ground. He pulled into the parking lot, sauntered up to the door and knocked. As he stood on the stoop, he brushed the light coating of snow from his hair, causing a cow lick to stand up at attention. The door opened.

"Hi, Veronica."

"Bobby? Oh, hey, come in! I didn't expect to see you. Sorry, the place is a real mess."

"That's okay. Messes aren't a problem for me."

"Here, let me take your coat. Geez, I can't believe it's snowing already. I must really be out of it today. I was just watching this stupid movie on TV. Just bein' a slug...I haven't done much else as you can obviously see."

"Really, that's fine. I'm here to see you, not your dishes."

"Are you sure, because they're all there in the sink waiting for an audience," she laughed.

"No, no, it's fine. I just need to talk to you about something. Do you have a minute?"

"Sure. I have a lot of minutes. That's what the pause button on the remote is for."

Bobby sat down on a hard wooden chair across of the couch. He couldn't quite put his finger on it, but interacting with Veronica felt awkward and forced today, much different than how his talk with Shondra began.

"Okay, so what's up?"

"Well, uh, we've been seeing each other for, what, like three months now?"

"Four," she corrected him.

"Yeah, alright, four. And, I really think things are going pretty well, don't you?"

"Yeah, why wouldn't I think so?"

"No, that's not what I meant. I was gonna say that, uh, I've been thinking about us..."

Veronica's posture became undeniably rigid. "Go on..."

"And, well, you know how everything's great and all. Well, I thought that maybe we could just start seeing each other. You know, exclusively. And not see anybody else."

Veronica furrowed her brow and cocked her head to one side, as if she was a confused puppy. "Uh, aren't we doing that now? Just seeing each other?"

"Well, I guess I was meaning that we could *officially agree* to be exclusive and not see other people anymore. You know what I mean?"

A very interesting look came over Veronica's face, an expression he'd never seen before. His initial hope was that this look meant something good, but in the next moment he realized how quickly things were about to escalate, and not in a good way.

"Not see other people? *Really?* Are you telling me that you have been seeing other people all this time? Over the past four months? Because I sure the fuck haven't been. I thought that you and I *were* exclusive already. See, just because I work at a strip club doesn't automatically mean that I fuck around on guys when I start to date them. But apparently *you* do and have done so since I met you."

Bobby stood up and put his hands out in an attempt to calm Veronica down. She was already pacing back and forth in front of the window.

"No, Veronica, that's not what I meant at all. I mean... well, I didn't think..."

"No, I guess you didn't think, Bobby. I guess you assumed that all the dancers at Bickley's like to fuck like rabbits and that's why they're working there. What, is it like a brand new menu every day? I figured some of the other guys working there were like that, but I swear I never thought *you* were."

"I'm not, Veronica, I'm really not. You're not understanding me."

"No, actually, I think I am. Let me guess, some other girl told you to piss off and now you want to have a 'sure thing'. Uh, I don't think that's going to happen. Let me make this real easy on you. You and your cast of sluts can go directly to hell and leave my house and not call me again. How's that for exclusive?"

He went over to her, trying to stop her frantic pacing. As he reached for her shoulders, she knocked his hands away.

"Veronica, please listen to me. You've got this all wrong. You don't understand."

"Okay. Fine," she stated and planted herself in front of him. "Then answer this question. Since we've been going out, have you seen anyone else?"

"I see lots of people every day," he smirked.

"Do you see me laughing at that? You think this is all a big joke or something? Answer me. Have you seen any other *girl* in the past four months? And you know what I mean by 'see'."

Bobby looked at the ground. He felt a little lost with no blanket thread to pull.

"Well, I, uh…I didn't realize that you wanted to be so serious at the beginning and…"

"Ugh, stop. Just stop. Don't try to explain or weasel out of it or come up with some stupid story about just being friends with someone else. Just…God, just leave. Don't call me or text me or anything."

"What about Bickley's?"

"What *about* Bickley's? I was working there before you were. If anything, *you* should be the one to leave."

"Wait. I don't have to quit my job just because you happen to work there, too."

"Well, do whatever you want. You obviously have been all along."

"Veronica, I really like you. I don't want us to end like this."

"Okay, Bobby. I'll ask again. Have you been seeing anyone else over the past four months? It's not a hard question. Either yes or no."

"Sort of."

"G'bye, Bobby. You know where the front door is. Use it."

CHAPTER 23

FISHIN'

▲ ▲ ▲

LEONARD AND PHIL SPENT A sweaty fifteen minutes bundling themselves up in parkas, rubber boots, layers of wool scarves and heavy duty winter gloves. The scarves covered most of their faces and the sunglasses hid the rest so anyone passing by might be able to make out part of a nose, if that. They hadn't gone ice fishing for some time, but that day everything fell perfectly into place: schedules, weather, ice, and allowances from wives. Phil had suggested that they head over to Perillo's Lake, a fifty minute drive from Badfish, and Leonard jumped at the opportunity.

His real intent wasn't necessarily fishing; it was to keep Phil company. He loved the sport, but *ice* fishing could be tough on his arthritis. If they actually managed to snag a fish or two during their outing, it would be a bonus.

Phil drove his pick-up truck over to Leonard's house bright and early. Leonard's wife, Gertie, never could understand why the fish got up so early themselves.

"Why wouldn't they want to sleep in? Give those poor creatures a break and let them catch a few more winks before you go swinging worms in front of 'em," she would say.

As the men pulled in to the lake parking lot, they saw other fishermen packing up their gear.

"What gives, fellas?" Leonard called out as Phil started to unload the truck.

"Ice is too thin. Warming up too fast today," one of the men shouted back.

"Really? We heard it was gonna be about twenty degrees today and tomorrow."

The man yelled once more as he closed his trunk. "You can try it, but I wouldn't advise it."

"Thanks for the tip," Phil added, waving. "Well, partner, what do you want to do now? We've got the day open with no women folk around."

"Well, when life gives you lemons...," Leonard started, but Phil cut him off.

"You go eat breakfast. Good idea."

▲ ▲ ▲

Twenty minutes later, they pulled into the parking lot of *Joe n' Joe*, a coffee and Sloppy Joe joint that Phil had discovered the last time he drove through the area. They hopped out of the pick- up, went in and were immediately led to a quiet four-top near the back. The table faced a window that looked out over a field behind the restaurant.

A waitress named Scooby took their drink orders and left them with a two page paper menu that had been trapped in plastic. She also pointed out the day's special; fried catfish.

"Does she have to rub it in about *fish?*" Phil snickered when she left their table.

"Aw, come on. Forget about it. We'll just have a reason to come back here in December, that's all."

They shared a laugh and studied the menu. When Scooby returned, they had decided on the Mornin' Joe plate. Phil wanted extra biscuits, but Leonard was happy with the two that already came with it. A coffee refill later, Scooby left to place their order with the kitchen, leaving the two men to themselves.

"So tell me, Leonard. When are you gonna quit that silly job of yours at the Finchon and retire once and for all?"

"Yeah, I know. The wife and I have been talking about that very thing lately. At first, I really needed the extra money. You remember that whole thing with the tire plant, how they screwed up our pensions all to heck."

"Oh, yeah. That was sheer lunacy what they did to us. I was lucky that my wife already had her pension from teaching."

"You *were* lucky, I'll tell ya. But I've been able to sock some away, make some decent investments. Nothing big mind you, but enough for me an' Gertie to be comfortable."

"Good for you, Leonard. I tell you, my hat is off to you for working at that motel practically every day. Everybody knows what kind of...people... it attracts these days. Hell, if I didn't know any better, I'd say that's ground zero for all the problems we've got going on in Badfish."

Leonard nodded. "Yep, I think so too. It wasn't so bad at first, right around the time that I started there. But between you and me, I'd say it's getting closer to being dangerous than just housing folks down on their luck these days."

"How so?"

"Well," Leonard hesitated. He sensed the need to be cautious with how much he really wanted Phil to know. "I don't want to spread rumors or anything, but let's just say that I don't feel as comfortable with some of the clientele as I once did."

Phil nodded and took a drink from his coffee. He added three more sugars to the remaining half cup.

"What do you mean, pal? Are you telling me that someone got violent with you?"

"No, nothing like that. It's just that there's a lot more drugs now. *Harder* people are staying there, you know? Phil, you remember years ago, right after Karl bought the place? How there were maybe a few homeless hanging out or people passing through the area staying there a week or two? Well, nowadays it's like there's more of a criminal element that's taken over. *That* and some other creepy stuff."

"Creepy? Now I'm really intrigued. Do you mean that you got ghosts up there at the Finchon?"

Leonard smiled. "Not exactly that kind of ghost, but some of them…geez…they might as well be zombies 'cause they look like the walking dead."

"What's Mr. Moneybags' take on all these clientele changes?"

Leonard cracked a tiny smile. He remembered his conversation with Karl about being a businessman versus not being one. He motioned for the waitress to bring them another coffee refill.

"Oh, that's simple. As long as Karl is making money, he doesn't care how it comes in."

"As long as it *keeps* coming in, huh? Yeah, I know the type."

"But, I tell you, I've gone over my accounts an' Gertie and I have been talking. Between the pension finally kicking in next year and our savings, I think I'll be able to retire for good this time."

"That would be great, buddy. We could go fishin' every day without having to worry about your work schedule."

"I think the wife gets first dibs on me, but I'll pencil you in as second on that list."

Scooby returned with two orders of *Mornin' Joe* and set them in front of each man. She said she would return with the extra biscuits as soon as they were done baking. Phil said that there was nothing better than hot biscuits right out of the oven and that he couldn't wait to load them up with butter and jelly. Apparently, that made Scooby so hungry, she reached down and broke off a piece of Phil's biscuit and ate it in front of him.

"Honey, you are so right. That is damn tasty. Hell, I'll bring you boys a bunch more of 'em, if I can smuggle 'em out before Mattie gets to 'em again."

"Who's Mattie, the other waitress?"

"No; the owner's dog."

Leonard and Phil gave each other a dumbfounded look and turned back to Scooby, but she had already walked back into the kitchen with the other half of Phil's biscuit.

"Okay, Phil, you owe me for this one," Leonard laughed. "I thought you said this place was a good find."

"Let's just say the more I learn about this little hidden gem, the less I want to know."

Both men laughed and started in on their breakfast. Regardless of what shenanigans were going on in the kitchen, they were hungry and the smell of hot food overpowered whatever reservations they had about the cleanliness of the restaurant.

"So, do you have a date in mind?" Phil asked, wiping his mouth with a napkin. "About retiring?"

"I'm shootin' for the last day in December."

"New Year's Eve? Wow, that's brave, buddy. Does your boss know yet?"

Leonard shook his head and put his knife and fork down. He took a big breath, held it for a second and let it out slowly before he answered.

"No, Phil, he doesn't. The only people that know about this are me, my wife, and now you. I know that my wife and I can keep this a secret, but I gotta say that I'm a little worried about *you*."

"What? What are you saying, Leonard? We've been friends for how long? You think I'm a blabbermouth?"

"Well, you do have a reputation of bein' the town crier, my friend."

"I'm not gonna say a word about this to anyone. I know how important this is to you. Now, can I have your other biscuit?"

CHAPTER 24

LIONFISH LOUNGE

▲ ▲ ▲

TRACY SET THE SECOND BLENDER next to the growing collection of dirty glassware that had started to accumulate ever since the well dressed couple at the far end of the bar had showed up. Apparently, testing Tracy's bartending skills and complaining about everything was high on their 'entertainment for the day' list. They seemed to enjoy tormenting the help. Tracy already overheard the two of them consorting with each other about experiencing the seedier side of the area before leaving. *For shits and giggles*, the man chuckled.

The moment the couple sat down, the suited man held up his hand and snapped his fingers without even looking in Tracy's direction. When she asked to take their order, neither he nor the woman made eye contact, but insisted that she use *clean* glasses when serving them. Before she left to mix their drinks, Tracy placed a bowl of peanuts and popcorn in front of them. The couple stopped their private conversation in mid-sentence, exchanged wide-eyed looks with each other and laughed.

"Uh, I don't think so. We're not eating anything from here," the man scoffed. "Just the drinks, and please hurry. I can feel my I.Q. drop the longer we sit here." The woman laughed at her husband's feeble attempt at humor.

Tracy held her tongue. It pained her to have to hold back the urge to say something snarky in return, but she didn't want a good zinger to be the reason she lost a job. Instead, she focused on making the drinks as quickly as possible and served them in the same manner. It took her three tries to make the something that this couple found acceptable.

She was also tending to the handful of customers at the other end of the bar when two strippers from Bickley's entered. Each woman was dressed as if she was about to take the stage – four inch high heels, sheer red stockings with garters and a leather bustier. Whether they were actually coming from or going to work wasn't clear. What *was* clear was the fact that they had been into something before visiting Lionfish Lounge. Their slurred speech and sloppy gaits were dead giveaways.

"Hey Bailey, Evey," Tracy shouted above the other conversations in the bar. "Looks like you guys found a heck of a party. Sorry I missed it. Can I get you anything, like some hot coffee or an ice pack for your future hangovers?"

"Tracy!" Evey screamed. "How the hell have you been?! Oh, my God, it's been like, what, a week since we've seen you? We love you so much; will you come home with us?"

Tracy stifled a laugh. Every week for the past two years, Bailey and Evey would stop in the Lounge, order one overly sweetened drink, and nurse it over the course of an hour while they regaled Tracy with tales about working at Bickley's. Most of the stories revolved around some of the trolls they met. To the staff at Bickley's, a troll was just another word for dirty old man who should know better.

The best story in recent history was the time that Donald Bickley was watching his prized possession, Nina, gyrate and grind on stage during one of her sets. It was common knowledge with the locals that Donald Bickley masturbated while he watched the dancers. With this bit of information, most of the regulars gave him a wide berth when they saw him in the back of the room.

As Evey told it, Donald was in his usual spot behind the bar, jerking away when all of a sudden a spray of beer from a popped keg doused him, most of the bar and pissed off some guys sitting a couple of yards away. The dancers thought the whole thing was pretty hilarious, but Bickley stormed away to his office and no one saw him for the rest of the day.

Tracy didn't think that the women were much into storytelling on this particular evening. Something about them was a bit off.

"I've been good, but not as good as you guys are doing. Are you starting your weekend early or continuing from the last one?" Tracy asked, setting two cold waters in front of them.

"That is perfect," the well dressed woman smirked. "Look at those cheap hookers drunk already. That is truly the epitome of a place like Badfish, isn't it? Damn, I wish I had my camera, but I think I left it in the suitcase."

"Here, I've got my phone. Let me get this," the man added, clicking away.

Bailey was the first to notice the sudden photo shoot. She turned halfway around in her seat and frowned.

"Hey. You assholes got a problem? Don't fuckin' take our pictures."

"What? It's a free country. We can take pictures of our surroundings if we want."

Bailey stumbled off the bar stool and took a step toward the couple. "Not if it involves me n' Evey. Gimme that phone."

The man stood up and held the phone out of reach as if keeping a toy away from a toddler.

"Why don't you go back to your ho' friends and drink the day away until your pimp daddy calls you?"

"Fuck you, dickhead!" Bailey charged toward him swinging her fists wildly, but the man side-stepped her. Everyone watched her bounce off of his bar stool and fall to the ground.

"Oh, shit." Tracy ran around from behind the bar. "Bailey, are you okay?"

Bailey moaned and put her hand to her head. She felt a small bump that would turn into an ugly, discolored goose egg before the end of the day.

Tracy turned her attention to the couple who were in the process of gathering up their things to leave.

"You! Hold it right there. I'm not done with you guys. I'm calling the police."

The man and woman stopped donning their coats and hats and looked around the bar. All eyes were on them.

"What would be the point, may I ask? That a couple of hookers got their feelings hurt and a bartender in an ass-backwards town was offended? Go ahead and call them if you want, but we're leaving."

"*Don't* leave a tip, dear," the woman whispered.

"What about their right to privacy? You can't just go around taking pictures of people without their permission."

"Yeah, you tell 'em," Bailey mumbled as she hoisted herself up off the floor with Tracy's help.

"And slander and bullying," Tracy added. She grasped for legal terms she had heard on Judge Judy.

"Nice try. We're done here," the man stated. He dropped a $5 bill on the bar and began to escort his wife to the door.

Evey ran in front of the couple. Her arms were crossed, her eyes were open wide and rivulets of frothy foam dripped from her lips. A peculiar sound emanated from her body as she began to shiver.

"I suggest you move aside and keep your hands to yourself," the man barked as he hooked his arm around his wife's shoulders.

"Shhtp."

The man called over his shoulder toward Tracy and Bailey. "Would you kindly remove your friend from the doorway so we can leave this pit?"

"Oh, I guess she's too disgusting to touch, right? You might catch something from us?" Bailey spewed. She tried to walk toward the couple, but Tracy held her back.

"Evey, just let them leave, okay? I don't want to have to get the police here and go through all that. Karl would have a fit if this turned into a big scene."

"Shhhtp, youuu," Evey burbled, then lunged at the woman.

The entire bar erupted into chaos. Bystanders suddenly jumped in, attempting to break up the cat fight. Tracy let go of Bailey and ran to the phone behind the bar to call the police, allowing Bailey to melt back down onto the floor in a drunken stupor. The well dressed man tried to wedge himself in between Evey and his wife, but somehow got knocked out of the way. This fight was personal.

"Youuu biatchh," Evey yelled and began to shake the woman violently. Her vice-like grip on the woman's shoulders punctured through her coat, then her wool sweater and finally her skin and muscle. Evey forcefully whipped her back and forth, making the woman look like a bobble-head doll.

The woman screamed in pain and anger. She grasped Evey by the wrists and yanked down as hard as she could in order to dislodge herself from this wild beast. When she pulled on Evey's arms, only her skin came off; the bone, muscles and tendons remained.

Both women shrieked in horror and disgust. The well dressed woman looked down into her own hands which now held two sheaves of someone else's skin. She stepped back and vomited. Evey looked to see her own skin molting off of her body. She raised her hands to her head just in time to catch her face which had dislodged itself and was literally falling off of her skull.

Every customer in the bar either ran out or passed out from shock. Tracy dropped the phone to the floor, frozen with fear. She stood, motionless as she watched the rest of Evey's flesh slide off into a hideous pile of rose colored tissue. The remains of Evey crumpled to the floor in a ghastly pile of blood, guts, bones, muscles and nerves just as Karl walked through the front door of the Lounge.

CHAPTER 25

KARL'S THIRD MEETING

▲ ▲ ▲

"You son-of-a-bitch, Manny. Now I've got the fuckin' police sniffing around in my shit. You told me…you gave me your word that this kind of thing would not happen again. Do you have any idea what kind of hell I walked into over at the Lionfish? A fuckin' shitstorm, that's what. And do you know what I'm thinking at that moment? Let me tell you. I'm thinking that the next time I see Manny Estovar, I'm gonna put a bullet in his head and take my business elsewhere."

"No, no, no, please. I can explain."

"We've had this discussion already. I thought I was very clear about this. I don't give a shit what's in the product or what it does or who the hell shoots up with it. The only thing that I *do* give a shit about is not being the one left cleaning up the aftermath and having to answer damn questions from the cops. But what do you think I did this afternoon? Tell me, Manny, what the hell did I do earlier today, right before I called your ass?"

"Clean up aftermath?"

Karl took a key out of his pocket and unlocked his desk drawer. He reached in and pulled out a Beretta Tomcat and aimed it at Manny's head. Manny instantly dropped to the ground. He cowered and begged him to put the weapon away. Instead, Karl kicked the chair aside and placed the barrel of the gun on the top of the whimpering man's head.

"Why should I give you another chance? What, to fuck me over again? So the cops can run background checks and close my business? So I can be stuck in endless investigations for years, if not longer? What are you doing to me, Manny?"

"Please, no, Karl. Give me a chance to go back to my supplier and talk to him. I'll make this right, I promise. Please, please don't shoot me."

"How's your memory, Manny? Do you remember the last time we had one of these special meetings in this office? Do you recall what I said to you at that time? Let me refresh your memory. I said that if we had to have this particular chat again, that it would be our last meeting. Remember that?"

"Karl, please. If you kill me, the cops will trace it back to you. Come on, I'm beggin' you, please don't do this."

Karl stepped back but kept his finger on the trigger. He stood quietly and watched Manny slowly bring his arms down from his head and wipe the sweat from his face. Karl contemplated what his next step should be, both as a businessman and as someone who didn't want to end up in prison.

The last thing he needed was a loose end; someone he couldn't trust. The drug dealers he had previously dealt with had been seedy, but he never had problems like the ones he was dealing with now. Manny had been a liability from the word go.

Teaming up with Manny was never in Karl's original plans. Keith O'Bannon, Karl's original drug contact, always came through and for a while everything worked. When the tourists stopped coming to the Finchon, the number of transients and addicts went up, and they were bringing friends. The rooms were full and the money continued to roll in. The quality of O'Bannon's supply was solid. But after Keith suddenly got busted for a charge that had nothing to do with peddling dope, Karl was desperate for someone to fill the position.

When Manny took over and brought his own special supplier with him, the problems began. People started dying in the most monstrous ways, and now the police were involved. No amount of under-the-table payoffs would make this go away.

Yes, Manny was most definitely a liability.

"You know what, Manny? You're absolutely right. If I kill you, that might cause a lot of problems for me. And at this point, the last thing I need is more problems. So, I tell you what. Today is your lucky day. I've chosen not to kill you."

"Oh," Manny breathed a huge sigh of relief, "thank you. Thank you! Karl, you are doing the right thing. You have my sincere word; I will make this up to you. I will have a very serious talk with my supplier and tell him that this cannot happen again. Thank you so, so much."

Karl reached into the top drawer of his desk, took something out and hid it behind his back.

"Don't thank me yet. You've proven that I can't trust you. You don't have my best interests at heart because you continued to supply me with shit that ends up hurting my bottom line. And you should know by now that if someone fucks with my bottom line, *that someone* has to pay. I could tell you to get the hell out of here and just call someone else, which, by the way, I will be doing. But you brought so much of that crap into Badfish, it's gonna take a long time for that garbage to cycle itself out of here. And while I'm waiting for that to happen, I'll still be cleaning up your aftermath."

"It doesn't have to be like that, Karl. I'll stop bringing that stuff this second, man. Consider it done, *this very second*."

"Not good enough. That orange shit is all through this town. Sure, you might be able to stop any *new* supply, but that bullshit is *already here*."

"But...but I-" Manny started to stand but Karl stepped forward. He cringed back down onto the floor.

"None of this will be a concern for you anymore. And I'm not even going to shoot you."

"I don't understand."

"It's simple. Your death will look like just another overdose at the Finchon."

In one swift move, Karl plunged the syringe he had been hiding behind his back into Manny's neck. The fluorescent liquid flowed from the vial into the man's body, causing instant spasms. Manny looked up at Karl, stunned and horrified. Neither man knew how his body would react to this drug. There had been dozens of people with different reactions, but all of them ended in death.

Manny jumped up and tried to wipe the shot off of his neck, but the drug was already racing through his veins. Sweat poured down his face. He thought it was the tension of the situation, but realized that his body was simply reacting to what it had been fed. He ripped off his clothes as the perspiration leaked from every cell. Standing naked in the middle of Karl's office, Manny continued to wipe down his arms, face, and torso, but he couldn't keep up. He threw his drenched clothes into the corner. He grabbed a cup off of Karl's desk and dumped it over his head, not caring if it were cold water or hot coffee.

A putrid smell suddenly doused the office. Karl backed up against the far wall, captivated by this gruesome show. Manny's bowels loosened all over the floor; the contents of his bladder followed. Karl put his hand over his nose and mouth, yet kept his eyes on the man liquefying in front of him. Manny grimaced and grabbed his abdomen. He felt a boiling pressure inside his gut. Throwing up wasn't an option as his intestines began streaming out of his anus and piling up next to the mound of steaming feces. His stomach and other internal organs dropped out next, adding to the array of grotesque colors and textures on the floor. As he opened his mouth to speak, a flood of orange goo spewed out from his nose instead. His eyes; first the right, then the left, melted down his cheeks in a white and brown-flecked stream. The rest of his body collapsed; a pile of quivering slush finally coming to a complete rest. A waft of steam escaped the heap of mush in a whispery sizzle, and then fell silent.

Karl approached the remains carefully. He studied it, still protecting his nose and mouth with his hand. He turned away and went to the window that overlooked the highway. The Finchon sign had just blinked to life; its neon letters glowed against the evening sky. The green chevron pointed inward toward the buildings, a signal to weary travelers in search of a comfortable respite. A siren song to the masses, that they might find peace and quiet within this establishment.

He watched a few cars drive past the motel. He turned around and took a step closer to what had once been a human being. Speaking through his hand, he said, "I told you I wasn't done cleaning up from you."

Karl picked up the phone and dialed.

"Leonard, I need you to come in tonight."

CHAPTER 26

DECEMBER

▲ ▲ ▲

THE FIRST DAY OF DECEMBER brought a cold, snowy front with it. There was a sharp chill that ran through the town of Badfish, a feeling which travelers almost seemed to sense. Those looking for a place to stay quickly bypassed the small town in search of other lodging.

On that first day of the month, the Finchon stood at ninety percent capacity, full of addicts, transients, and strip club dancers. The Lionfish Lounge still had its share of customers; regulars or people passing through town, stopping to grab a quick bite to eat. The biggest draw continued to be Bickley's. Those who visited the club several times a week either lived in Badfish or in one of the surrounding towns.

Karl hated that Donald Bickley made more money than he did. He often thought about the irony of it; that a queer like that son-of-a-fag Bickley would have balls enough to run a titty bar. If anyone would, it should have been Karl. *A fucked up version of Monopoly if there ever was one*, he would say to Leonard. It was almost enough of an irritant to push Karl into actually upgrading his businesses.

As he stewed behind the customer service desk mulling it all over in his mind, Karl picked up the phone and called Leonard, who was home at the time.

Leonard and his wife hadn't left the house to go Christmas shopping for the grandkids yet. He was still fumbling around with three different shopping lists and a pile of coupons as he mindlessly felt for his tweed hat among the mittens and scarves on the top shelf of the closet. Once his head was sufficiently covered, he reached over to pick up the car keys off of the little table in the hall. The phone rang at the same moment.

"Hello?"

"Leonard? I need you to come in."

Leonard looked at his wife who had one foot on the front stoop and the other in their entryway. She gave him the 'if it's not important, let's go' look. He waved his hand at her. He understood and agreed.

"Um, sorry boss, not this time. The wife and I are walkin' out the door this very minute."

"Not the answer I want. I need you over here now. I've got some ideas and I don't want this to wait until Monday. You can be here in about ten minutes, right?"

"Karl, I told ya, I can't do this today. It's my day off and the wife and I got plans. I'll see you tomorrow and we can talk about whatever you want then."

"Dammit, Leonard, I'm not *asking* you. I'm telling you to get your ass over here now. If you plan on keeping your job after today, then I'll see you in a few minutes," Karl barked and slammed the phone down.

Leonard jumped a little at the sound of the receiver hitting its base. He looked over at his wife who, without saying a word, nodded and began taking off her matching hat, scarf and mittens.

"Dear, I-I don't know what to say here," Leonard said.

"Go on, it's fine. We can go later today. There's still enough time to get everything and have it shipped to the kids. But I think you ought to have that talk with Karl. You know the one I mean. It's high time he knows that he won't be able to order you around anymore after the first of the year. I say good riddance to bad karma."

"Well, I wasn't planning on leaving on such a bad note. Why don't I run over there now and see what all his yammerin' is about. I should be back by two at the latest."

"Not a minute longer, Leonard, or I'll come down there myself and give him a piece of my mind."

"No, no, no…," Leonard laughed, "he couldn't handle dealing with the *big guns*."

She smiled, sat down at the kitchen table and snapped the newspaper open to the leisure section.

▲ ▲ ▲

Karl stared at the clock on the wall; his arms folded across his chest while beads of sweat rested on his upper lip. When Leonard walked in, brushing off snowflakes from his coat sleeves, Karl locked eyes with him.

"That was more like twenty."

"Pardon me?"

"Twenty minutes. I expected you in ten."

"You're wound kind of tight today, boss. Tell me, what was so important that I had to come down here on my day off? Wait; before you do, let me just tell you that your demands today didn't make a fan out of my wife. Why, she told me before I left that if I wasn't home by two-o-clock, that she would head over here and give you what for," Leonard smiled good-heartedly.

"Leonard, why do you insist on defying me? If I didn't fuckin' need you here, I wouldn't have called you. Don't you realize that I gave you a job when no one else would? At your age, you're damn lucky that *anyone* hired your ass, yet here you are complaining when I ask you to do something."

Leonard was taken aback. Karl had never spoken to him that harshly before. He was used to Karl's snarky attitude and under the breath grumbling, but he never jumped down his throat with such disdain. Leonard was about to brush it off like he always had, just roll with the punches, so to speak, but he thought about the conversation with his wife just before he left the house.

She was right. I shouldn't be talked down to like this. I'm a good employee and he's been taking advantage of my good nature for a long time. There's no reason for such rudeness, especially when I showed up on my day off. I've come in at the drop of a hat when he needed his garbage cleaned up; those poor, desperate folks that got hooked on Karl's monstrous drugs. He wouldn't dare get his fancy clothes defiled by touching the horrors that I've had to deal with. All that gets dumped at my feet while my wife sits at home alone by herself. Well, enough is enough.

"Leonard, did you hear me?"

"Actually, Karl, for the first time, I think I really did."

"What's that supposed to mean?"

"It means I quit. Here, here's my name tag and if you'll give me a minute, I'll get the keys off my key ring," Leonard said.

He unlatched the supervisor's key and placed it on the customer service counter.

"I can't very well say that it's been a pleasure to work for you, but it *was* a paycheck and for that, I do appreciate it. Don't worry about me telling anyone what I've been witness to here. I'd just as soon forget all that than bring it up to the police. I'll come by in a couple of weeks and get my final paycheck…well, wait a minute. Why don't you just mail it to the house? I think that'll work out better for everyone involved, don't you? I don't plan on stepping foot in this place again. I think that covers everything. Good luck to ya. From what I've seen, I think you're going to need it."

As he finished his speech, Leonard pulled his cap down and adjusted his scarf in preparation for the cold waiting for him outside. He opened the office door a final time, held up a hand as a gesture of farewell and walked out of the Finchon.

Karl didn't move. He couldn't. Leonard's retort had left him speechless and defenseless, but after the initial shock had passed and the scope of what just happened had a chance to sink in, Karl went into his office and shut the door, leaving the customer service counter empty.

He unlocked a desk drawer and reached into the back. He pulled out a small metal flask. Karl wasn't an alcoholic, but in one swift gulp, he emptied the entire contents of the curved container, screwed the cap back on, and threw it across the room. He kicked his chair, which sent it flying into a file cabinet, knocking over piles of papers. He shoved his large desk to the wall, giving flight to receipts and folders. He toppled the other two cabinets, dumping their contents onto the floor. A baseball bat that he kept for protection rested in one of the corners. He picked it up and threw it against the confines of the room, just missing the window.

Finally, he crumpled to the floor and let go a large, pitiful sob. He held his head in his hands, rubbed his eyes, massaged his face, and screamed out loud.

"Fuck Leonard! Fuck him and fuck his cunt of a wife! I don't need him. I never needed him. I don't fuckin' need anybody. I can do whatever the fuck I want!"

He looked around at the disaster he created. Eyeing the phone which was overturned near one of the cabinets, he reached over to grab the receiver and dialed a number.

"Westin Movers. How can I help you today?"

"Is Marc Wegan there?"

"Marc? Yeah, hold on; let me get him for you."

"Hello, this is Marc Wegan."

"Wegan, its Karl. I need your help."

CHAPTER 27

BOBBY PRICE

▲ ▲ ▲

BOBBY PRICE SAT ON HIS bed with a small calculator on his left and a pile of paycheck stubs on his right. A notebook rested in his lap, its pages filled with simple math equations and schedules. Some of the tabulations had been completely scratched out, while others had boxes and stars next to them.

Bobby hadn't seen G-Force in about a week, which was strange, even for him. Usually, by this time of the afternoon, G would have knocked, entered without being asked, and given Bobby the peace sign. Then, he would scour the room for any hint of food that happened to be out in the open. Bobby learned early on to hide anything edible. He knew that if G even saw so much as a crumb, it would be gone. The man had never been shy about taking what he wanted, even if it didn't belong to him.

The lack of G's visit was of little concern to Bobby at this point. While it was true that without it he wouldn't have enough product to move over the coming weekend, Bobby had gotten better at saving. If he had his finances figured out correctly, he was actually in pretty good shape. Having double checked his math, he realized if he could pick up about six more hours a week at Bickley's, he wouldn't have to deal with the drugs at all.

The allure of the orange liquid was not only frustrating, but mystifying at the same time. He wasn't a stranger to pot and had tried a little bit of cocaine a few years ago, but he never really went in for the whole drug scene. Yet, here he was working in a strip club and selling drugs to the clientele, living the ultimate cliché.

When he left his parents' house at seventeen, Bobby didn't have any particular goal in mind other than to get out from under someone else's rules. He and a couple of buddies rented a double-wide that wasn't anything more than a roof out of the rain, but it worked for a while. Fast food jobs and sweeping floors took them through the better part of two years, but living by the seat of their pants lost its charm every time the bills were due. Eventually, Bobby decided to opt out of the following year's contract and moved an hour south to Badfish. He figured he could find a decent job, settle down and raise a family -- a dream that he imagined most young men had at his age.

As time passed, he realized that he didn't want to spend the next thirty years of his life as a bouncer at Bickley's Strip Club. And he certainly didn't want to spend another year living at the Finchon.

The final straw for him was selling drugs. He often thought about the people he sold to and what might have happened to them. The end results that he *did* see would haunt him for years to come. He remembered the party with the bonfire and the way the man screamed as he lay across the flames. He thought about the room where some unfortunate soul spun into oblivion, the same night he met Shondra.

Bobby felt partially responsible for those deaths. Not because he sold drugs to those *particular* people, but because he was *involved*. When money and syringes would exchange hands, he would never truly know into whose arm the needles would be shot. It made him sick, mulling over the possibilities: a child haphazardly finding it on a table in a living room or a pregnant teen in search of a bigger high. And what in the hell was the magnetic pull that the drug had on *him*? Every time he saw it, he desired it. Every time he held it, he longed to jam it into his own body. Every time he sold it, he wanted to keep it for himself. He lost count of how many times he imagined sticking the needle into his arm, pressing the plunger and giving himself over to the warmth that would consume his being, sending him to fantastical places he could never dream of without it.

But all of that was propaganda and he knew it. He even helped perpetuate some of those very notions to unsuspecting buyers. How could he continue to do that and sleep at night? How could he take their cash, lie to their faces and tell them to come back when they wanted more?

Bobby got up from the bed and walked over to the mirror. He stared into it, examining his face, studying the person he had become. He searched his mind, trying to pinpoint a cause or a reason for this unacceptable turn of events in his life.

He thought about seeing Veronica for the first time at Bickley's and how pretty she was. He remembered hoarding money in order to ask her out, saving for months so he could take her to the nicest restaurant he knew. His thoughts then drifted to Shondra. It was one of the most bizarre ways to meet someone, but the immediate connection they had was impossible to deny. He recalled their times together, talking about the Finchon, walking around Badfish, watching bad television together. Shondra was special. She had plans for the future and was taking actions to see them through, qualities he really admired. That kind of wherewithal was pretty uncommon around here and he knew it.

Maybe. *Maybe* there was some way that they could have a future together. It would be a leap of faith, sure, *but why the hell not?* What had been his life up to this point but working at shitty jobs and selling drugs to unsuspecting customers? Would he look back on his life at eighty, if he even made it that far, and feel blessed or proud or whatever about the wonderful legacy he left in the world? He was only twenty-two; a lifetime of opportunities was possible if he had the guts follow through. What would he be missing out on if he didn't? Living in some shithole motel and hanging out with derelicts like G-Force? No. He needed to change things. Now.

Bobby threw on a tee-shirt, grabbed his wallet and keys and headed out the door. He walked directly over to Shondra's room and knocked loudly.

"Shondra? Are you home? I gotta talk to you." He continued to pound on the door.

"What the heck?" she claimed as she opened the door.

"Shondra, I have a plan and I think it can work. We can do this."

"Bobby Price, get in here," she laughed as she helped him brush the snow off of his bare arms and wet hair. "Look at you without so much as a coat or hat on."

She shut the door and went to the bathroom to get a towel.

"I've been thinking," he said, "and you're gonna think I'm crazy, but I'm not. I'm serious."

She handed him a large white bath towel. "Well, the crazy part is already true. It's like ten degrees outside and you're walking around like it's the middle of summer."

He dried his face and ran the towel over his hair which made it stick up in spiky points like a punk rock singer. She took the towel from him and tossed it in a corner. They sat on the bed and pulled a blanket around themselves, bundling up together.

"Okay, what's this crazy idea you have that almost gave you pneumonia?"

"We should move outta here. We should move and get better jobs and if that means leaving Badfish, so what? We could do it, Shondra. We could do it today."

She tilted her head and smiled. "Bobby Price, you are hilarious. Of course we should move out of the Finchon. *Every single person that lives here* should move out but that doesn't mean that it's really going to happen this very second."

"It *is* going to happen. I've been saving, Shondra, and I have a lot of money right now. We could pack up and leave Badfish and get a small apartment somewhere else and start over. And I don't mean live in some piece of shit motel. I mean a real apartment with heat and cable and a mailbox…an' everything that we don't have now."

"I like the way you think, Bobby, but come on. I can't afford a real place, an' you know that."

"I'm not going without you."

"I told you, I can't afford…," she started, but he cut her off.

"Yes, you can. I told you, I've been saving and I want you to come with me. I've got enough to get us started and between the two of us working, we can do this. Hell, Shondra, I think we can leave today."

"Today? Leave *today*? Is that what you're saying?"

"I knew you'd think I was wacko, but I am dead serious. Right this second, I have over six thousand dollars in cash. I'll pay off whatever we owe for the rest of this month so you don't have to worry about that. I say we load up our cars and take off right now. We can find a place to stay where you can go to school and keep doing your CNA job. I'll find something too. No more Bickley's. Something different. Something *better*. I don't know, maybe I'll end up taking classes and be a CNA too."

Shondra turned to face him directly. She held his hands and squeezed them gently.

"You *are* serious about this, aren't you?"

"Yeah, I am and I want to do it today before I get all chickenshit about it," he chuckled.

It took her a moment to collect her thoughts, but deep down, she knew that everything he said made sense. The Finchon was becoming more chaotic and it was no place to live for someone who was trying to make something out of their life.

"Let's do it, Bobby Price. Let's get the hell out of here right now."

He pounced off the bed, bright with excitement, pumping his fists in the air and shouted.

"Yes! Yes! We are so out of here! Woo!" He paraded around the room, whooping gleefully, laughing and smiling as hard as his face would let him.

Shondra laughed too. Bobby's excitement was palpable and contagious. She hopped up on the bed and started jumping up and down, shouting and hooting along with him until the people in the rooms next door started banging on the walls, yelling at them to *'shut the fuck up 'cause we're trying to sleep'.*

"Sleep? At four in the afternoon? Fuck it, we are so outta here!" Bobby shouted at the bare wall.

"Bobby Price, I'll see you in an hour," Shondra giggled. "Here, take this blanket with you."

He wrapped it around his body like a huge, ugly shawl.

"An hour or less!"

Shondra laughed again. "Just go, silly! We've got things to do!"

CHAPTER 28

NINA

▲ ▲ ▲

IT HAD BEEN WEEKS SINCE Nina had worked a shift at Bickley's. Finally, when she called Donald at the club instead of facing another awkward visit at his house, he explained that although he wasn't too happy with her attendance, or lack thereof, he would let it slide. After all, this was *Nina* he was reprimanding and when it came to her, he didn't mind breaking all his own rules.

Under the continued guise of being sick, Nina spent a lot of her free time with Karl. Most of their dinner or movie dates usually ended up at either his house or her motel room with her on the verge of passing out. She had a hunch that he might be drugging her drinks, but as long as he kept spending money on her and giving her gifts, why not ride it out?

Karl lavished her with extravagant meals, fancy clothes, new dance outfits and expensive jewelry. If he felt her up and got his rocks off while she was passed out, what did she care? She reasoned it away, believing that if she wasn't aware of it, it didn't really matter. And the best thing was that most of the gifts he gave her would last far longer than their tumultuous relationship. Still, she didn't like that there was something smarmy and underhanded about him. Even though he could be witty and charming *for a man of his age*, she always felt that something ugly was percolating just under the surface.

Over the past couple weeks, Karl had become impatient; quick to anger and even quicker to react. He told her that it had to do with his assistant quitting on him, but she suspected that wasn't the whole story. Normally, he didn't discuss business regarding the Finchon or the Lounge, which was fine in her book. The less she knew about what went on behind the scenes, the better. The few times he did, it was mostly mundane stories about running a motel and lounge. Nina would nod and smile and say 'uh huh' at all the right places, but she found those conversations dreadfully boring and pointless.

However, if being short-handed in the office was the true cause for his sudden outbursts, it shouldn't be an excuse for him to snap at *her*. She had nothing to do with his business affairs.

Nina planned to set him straight during dinner. She was not going to be treated poorly by him or any other man for that matter, and if he intended on seeing her again, he would best be served by keeping his attitude in check. And then, just to drive the point home, she would unbutton her shirt a little lower in order to remind him of what he would be missing if he didn't heed her warning.

At 5:45pm, there was a loud, forceful pounding at her door. Before she could answer it, Karl barged in. His face was red and sweaty, an odd combination to see against the coldness of December. She noticed that his shirt was untucked, his tie was askew and one of his pant cuffs was caught in an argyle sock.

"Are you ready?" Karl slurred.

"Not quite," she calmly stated and glanced at the clock next to her bed. "You said six."

"It is six. Let's go. We have reservations."

"It's not six and I'm not done with my hair yet."

Karl swore under his breath. Nina couldn't quite make out what he said, but she knew from the tone of his voice that it was something foul. He yanked the chair out from the small table, swung it around to straddle it, and grabbed something from the bed to wipe his face.

"Hey," Nina snapped, "that's my teddy, not a fuckin' towel." She ripped it away from him, tearing one of the arm straps in the process. "Fuck! You owe me for that, you ass."

"Fine, let's just go already. Jesus, how long does it take women to get ready to stuff their face? It's not like everyone hasn't seen you naked. What the hell difference does it make if your hair's a little messy?"

"Fuck you, Karl."

"Just hurry up."

Nina stomped off into the bathroom and slammed the door while Karl pulled a little flask out of his suit coat pocket and took a swig. He put the cap back on, tucked it away and wiped his mouth with his coat sleeve.

In the bathroom, Nina threw a tube of lip gloss on the ground and cussed under her breath. She was so furious and distracted by Karl's behavior, that when she reached for the curling iron, she grabbed the wrong end and burned her hand.

"Shit!"

She howled and dropped the appliance on the floor. Part of the metal heating element flew off and hit the toilet with a sharp clink.

"Damn it." She kicked the broken iron away in disgust. "Great, that's just fuckin' great."

She picked up one of her brushes and tried to fix the section that was uncurled. When she finished, she walked out to find Karl slumped over in the chair, asleep. She tip-toed over and kicked one of the legs of the chair. Her high heel slipped and ended up knocking into his shin, waking him with an unpleasant start.

"What the hell? Why are you kicking me?"

"Sorry, I meant to kick the chair, not you."

"What the fuck? Why are you kicking at me at all? *I'm* the one waiting, not you."

"You're sleeping and it's rude, that's all."

He rolled his eyes. He was about to add something snarky, but thought better of it.

Karl stood up and spun the chair back under the table. "Sorry. Are you finished dolling yourself up?"

"Yes, Karl. I'm dolled."

"Let's go, then. We'll be lucky to make it on time now."

▲ ▲ ▲

Karl and Nina arrived at Che Vert just in time. A well dressed valet ran from the front of the restaurant, offered his services and exchanged keys and tags with Karl. As the couple entered the restaurant, another man wearing a tuxedo greeted them, checked them in at the hostess stand and led them to a private table in a secluded nook. He handed each of them a menu and placed a wine list next to Karl. He explained that their waiter, a young man name René, would be with them momentarily and wished for them to have a most pleasant dining experience before leaving the table.

"Wow, this is pretty high class," Nina said, admiring the surroundings. "Awesome pick, Karl. This is really nice."

"I thought this would meet with your approval."

"Now, see. *Right there*. Why do you have to be so snippy with me all the time? All I said was how nice a place this was and you start in on me. What's that all about?"

"I told you, I've been under some stress lately."

"Yeah, well, we need to talk about…," Nina began to chastise Karl, but was interrupted by René and his requisite menu explanations. After they ordered drinks and listened to the eager young man describe the specials of the day, Karl and Nina were left alone again.

"Boy, everything sounds so good. I'm thinking about getting that one dish with the shrimp and lobster. What did he call it? Well, it sounded amazing, so, yeah, I think that's what I'll go with. What about you? What do you think you'll get tonight?"

"Laid," he smirked.

"Nice, Karl. That's really nice. Here we are in this fancy restaurant and you're being crude. Like I started to say before, I'm getting pretty sick and tired of that attitude and I think I deserve to be treated a hell of a lot better than that. So, here's the deal. Either you stop with the nasty comments and shitty attitude toward me or this is going to be our last date for a while. Hell, maybe even forever, I don't know."

"Bullshit. You can't keep your hands off me and you know it. Nina, I'm so damn head and shoulders above any of those losers down at Bickley's. I own two businesses in this town, Nina. *Two.* What do you think most of those dregs of society do when they're not wanking off in front of you, huh? You think they're running a company somewhere? Shit. Most of 'em live down at the fuckin' Finchon and if they don't, they're sittin' at home in front of their computer screens with one hand on their greasy mouse and the other hand on their slimy dick."

"You know, Karl, you're probably right. But look who's sitting next to me. *You. You're* the one who came after *me*, you know. You're the one who came over to my room with wine, begging me to go out with you. So, uh, maybe *you* belong in that group of guys you're talking about, because the way I see it, you apparently want to be in the company of a stripper, just like the rest of them."

Karl glared at Nina. In that moment, he hated her; outright loathed her. He forced himself to hold back the screaming desire to reach over and choke the very breath out of her. That bitch. *How dare she lump me in the same category as those scumbags at Bickley's. Doesn't she realize who I am and what I am capable of?*

The moment was stilted by the waiter's return.

"Have we decided what we would like to order?" René asked, pen and paper at the ready.

▲ ▲ ▲

Karl looked the bill over carefully; $172.49. He pulled out his wallet and slapped a credit card down on the tray. Nina had gone to the rest room, leaving Karl to pay the bill and finish his third Crown Royal and Coke. He knew he shouldn't drive, even if it *was* only a thirty minute trip back to Badfish, but he figured what the hell? *What's the worst that could happen?* That both of them die in a fiery car crash? And that would be a big loss to whom exactly?

Nina came back to the table and put her coat around her shoulders.

"It's getting kind of cold, don't you think?"

"Hmm, yeah, s'pose it is."

"Are you okay to drive?"

"Sure," he slurred. "I can handle it."

"I don't know, Karl. Maybe I should drive home. You don't look too good."

"I am the man and the man drives the woman home."

"Yeah, well, *this* woman wants to get home alive and in one piece. Give me the keys."

Half an hour later, Nina pulled the cherry red Aston-Martin into the Finchon parking lot. She shut the car off and handed Karl his keys. They slid out of the car and stood silently as the snow fluttered peacefully down on their heads.

"Well, uh, I think I'm gonna turn in. Thanks for dinner and everything. I-uh…yeah."

She gave up the conversation, realizing the pointlessness of it all. She turned to walk up the stairs to her room.

"Wait. Wait a minute. I never gave you your Christmas present," Karl muttered as he braced himself against his car. "You gotta let me at least do that, 'kay? You go on up to your room and I'll be up in a few minutes."

"Alright. I guess that would be okay. But you don't have to. It's not even Christmas yet."

"Hey," he swayed, moving away from the car, "it's December 17, close enough."

"Actually, it's December 14, but, whatever. See you in a few minutes then." She turned away from him and went to her room.

Karl stumbled into the office, startling Neil. Neil didn't mind Karl's sporadic interruptions at odd hours of the night. He was getting paid ten dollars an hour, cash under the table, and all the pot he and his buddies could want. What seventeen-year-old would turn down that kind of deal?

"Hey, Mr. Demetris. Didn't expect to see you here tonight. Everything okay?"

"I'm fine, kid, just mind your own business. I'll be outta here in a minute."

"No problem. Everything's been pretty quiet around here tonight."

"Good. Let's hope it stays that way."

Karl unlocked his office door, rummaged around his desk for a minute and came back out carrying a large paper bag. He eyed Neil; gawky, glasses, long brown hair, obvious battles with acne that had been fought and lost over most of his face. He was glued to some game on his phone and must have gone up a level at that very moment because a little, tinny voice cheered from the speakers.

"Cool. Papa Fiesta, dude," Neil smiled and showed the phone screen to Karl.

Karl sighed.

"Yeah, okay. Just make sure to lock up when you leave, alright?"

"Got it. Lock it down when I leave."

Karl walked out of the office, shaking his head. *Teenagers.*

Nina had changed into sweatpants and a tee-shirt. The last thing she wanted to do was to convey a message to Karl that there might be more happening than a simple gift exchange. She turned on the television and all the lights. She toyed with the idea about running the shower too, but thought that would probably be overkill.

She decided that the best way to handle this was to accept the present, thank him, and then ask him to leave, citing reasons like being tired or feeling ill or anything else that might pop into her head at that moment. The shorter the exchange, the sooner she would be done with him.

Nina knew that this probably meant the end of the dinners and gifts from Karl. After tonight, the gravy train would be pulling away from the building. He might even go so far as to kick her out of the Finchon, but that would be harder to pull off, especially since she was paid up through February and she had a written agreement to prove it. She would just have to go back to work at Bickley's. At least she would have Donald to fuel her financial desires.

Karl knocked timidly on her door, waiting outside in the cold for a proper invitation to come in.

"Come on in." She stepped aside and held the door open.

"Thank you, Nina," he said, with a bit of a slur to his words. "I appreciate you seeing me now."

"It's okay."

"Well, I know it's not quite Christmas, but I have a s-special gift for you. Here. I didn't have time to wrap it, so I hope you'll forgive the bag." He handed her the sack.

"Thank you," she said, tentatively. He was being overly polite, never a good sign from someone so moody. She sat at the table, opened the bag and pulled out a bottle with a big bow on it.

"That right there…that's a good year, ya know," Karl stated, pointing at the label.

"Thank you, Karl. Williams Selyem, 2008, Pinot Noir. Well, I don't know much about wines, but it looks really nice."

"You're lookin' at a hundred bucks worth of alcohol right there. Something like that isn't just 'good,' it's fan-fuckin'-tastic."

"Is it? Have you had this before?"

"No, ma'am, I haven't had the pleasure. I was hoping we could crack it open and indulge together. I just happen to have a bottle opener with me. May I?"

Nina furrowed her brow. This was supposed to be a five minute interaction, *if* that. She didn't like the sudden change in agenda.

"I thought you were stopping by for a minute, Karl, not the rest of the night. I don't know if I like this."

"Please, *indulge* me. One last glass of amazing wine between friends and then I'll leave. It's the least you can do after everything that's happened between us."

"Fine," she answered, kicking herself mentally for giving in. "But I'm serious – one drink and you're out the door. I mean it."

"Meaning taken and understood."

Karl put the bottle between his knees and carelessly shoved the point of the bottle opener into the cork. Nina cringed at what could have been a very unpleasant result for Karl's manhood. He grasped the opposing grips and pressed down, releasing the cork with a loud pop. Nina went to the bathroom to retrieve two plastic cups from the sink.

He tipped the bottle over the lip of her cup and then over his own. He filled each glass about half full and set the bottle down on the table. He raised his cup to make a toast.

"A toast. To beginnings and to endings; may they both go down as easy as this wine."

"To endings," Nina said, raising her cup and drinking the contents.

Karl put the plastic to his lips and coughed, spilling the wine all over himself. "Oh, shit! Look'it this. Fuck...my new shirt."

"Jesus, Karl. Maybe you've had enough to drink today, *you think?* Here, let me get you a towel before you start destroying my wardrobe again." Nina went back to the bathroom and snagged a hand towel. "You know, I'm going to need more towels after all of this."

Karl wiped himself off and nodded. "That's okay. I'll send Neil over with some extra for you."

He handed her back the towel and straightened his clothes. "Well...I, uh, guess I should get going, huh? Sorry. That wine is really expensive; I sure didn't mean to waste any of it."

"No, that's fine, don't worry about it."

"Um, well, this is awkward, isn't it? Kinda like we're breaking up or something."

"We *are* breaking up, Karl, and yes, you *are* making this awkward. Thank you for the wine and for dinner. I'm going back to work tomorrow, so I need to get some sleep, okay?"

"Of course. Don't let that wine go to waste, though. It's a good one. I-I guess I'll see you around, huh?"

"I still live here, so, yeah, I guess you will. Bye, Karl."

"Bye, Nina. Goodnight."

As he walked out the door, she instantly threaded the chain on the lock. It was still hanging by a nail, but at least the effort was made. She went around turning off the lights and the television and shut the curtains. She poured herself another cup of wine, sat on the bed and made a quiet toast to herself.

"This one is to me. For having to put up with so much shit from so many guys, just to make a fuckin' living. Cheers." She raised the cup, complimented her own persistence, and drank.

CHAPTER 29

BICKLEY'S

▲ ▲ ▲

DONALD BICKLEY SAT ALONE IN his office reviewing employee timesheets. He was trying to figure out how he could afford to hire more bouncers without going over his old budget. It wasn't necessarily the cost, but the irony was difficult to swallow — hiring guys to stand around and watch girls take their clothes off. He laughed to himself. *They should be the ones paying me for that privilege.* Donald scribbled a note to himself as a reminder to talk to Bobby Price and Doug Mason about increasing their hours.

A quiet scratching on the door caused him to look up from his paperwork.

"Hi...are you busy?"

"Nina," Donald smiled and stood up. "Please, come in and have a seat. How are you doing? Are you feeling better? Is everything okay now?"

"I'm fine, Mr. Bickley. Please, don't get up on my account," she begged.

Jesus, he was so *needy*.

"I just came in to tell you that I'm feeling lots better. I can even work tonight. See, I brought my costumes and everything," she said, holding up bits and pieces of material.

"Oh, that's wonderful. I can add you back on the schedule for this evening. I'll have to rearrange a little, but consider it done."

"Thanks. That would be really helpful. You know...money and all."

"I just hope you stay well. Do you, umm, do you *need* more money?"

"Like, right now?"

"Sure right now," Karl said. He fished for the tiny key in his shirt pocket.

"Oh, uh, no. No, not this second. I'm good."

"Well, okay. Just let me know if I can help. I'm here for you, Nina. I want you to know that. I...uh...we missed you around here. It's not the same without you."

"Well, it's nice to be missed, I guess. But I'm back and ready to make some dough again. I'm gonna catch up with the other girls. Thanks again, Mr. Bickley."

And in the blink of an eye, Nina was out the door.

"At least she's back. I knew she couldn't stay away from me," he said, grinning.

▲ ▲ ▲

While Electra, whose real name was Nancy Turner, was dancing to her last song of the set, Nina finished adjusting the final touches of her costume; putting tassels in the most private of places. She only had about three minutes left before she had to go on, so she took the opportunity to unzip her backpack and grab the bottle of pinot noir from the night before. She chugged down the rest of it before jamming a small piece of cork back into the neck and hiding the empty bottle under a sweatshirt in her bag.

Nina heard the DJ thank Electra for her riveting performance and remind any fans that she would be doing her next set around eleven. A smattering of applause followed the announcement. In the next moment, *her* name rang through the speaker system which was followed by another weak round of applause. Her entrance music began.

She jogged out from stage left in her high heels, paused to center herself for a moment and then sauntered out to the middle of the stage. The spotlight hit her sharply in the eyes, blinding her. The music swept through the audience, swirled around the room and washed over her. The familiarity of her songs should have been routine, yet she found the music difficult, almost impossible to recognize. The melodies sounded muffled and muddied and the words came at her like an angry exotic language.

The men at the tables and the edge of the stage appeared as if they were covered in a gauzy haze. As she started to move and gyrate to the unearthly sounds pouring into her ears, the faces in front of her took on misshapen and distorted forms. The men closest to the front of the stage held their hands out, dollar bills clenched between moist, grimy fingers. However, in *Nina's* eyes, they didn't look like hands *or* bills *or* men for that matter. In her mind, she was surrounded by fleshy slug-like creatures, mutants that extended their tentacles forward in order to fuse themselves to her body. The more the men hooted and called for her, the more disconnected she felt to reality.

What the hell is happening? Why are these things watching me? What am I doing here and why am I wearing these clothes? These aren't mine. What is that noise and why won't it stop? Monsters...oh, God, they're monsters...I'm on display...oh my God, it's an auction. They're bidding on me. These human slugs are yelling.. Help, somebody...why are they pushing me back up here? I don't want to be here...

Nina stumbled back and forth on the stage, trying to hold on to the pole while attempting to balance against the chair. The men had now gone from hoots and cat calls to booing and shouting at her to get off the stage. They didn't want to see a drunken whore stumbling around.

Someone threw a crumpled up napkin; then a straw. Then, a wave a cherry pits and pretzels bombarded her, making her cry out in pain. A few of the men cussed and demanded their money back, trying to grab dollars off of the stage and out of her garter belt.

Stop it! Why are they pelting me with acid? It hurts! It burns! Why am I naked? Where are my clothes? Oh, God, the monsters are coming for me!

One of the bouncers jumped up on to the stage to try and shield Nina from the cascading debris being thrown at her, but that only made the audience boo louder. A couple of men rushed the stage and ripped off the rest of her costume in order to get a quick feel and a souvenir from 'the crazy stripper'. Nina made a feeble attempt to run off the stage, but the bouncer held her tightly, trying to calm her down. Somebody threw their drink, then another and another, until the floor was coated with watered down liquor and partially melted ice cubes.

As the bouncer and Nina struggled against each other, both their footing and their balance began to falter. They slipped and slid all over the stage, pushing each other into the chair and then the pole. The audience started chanting, yelling out either *bouncer* or *stripper*, depending on which side they were rooting for at that moment.

Monster...going to kill me! This thing wants my flesh! I can hear them all screaming for my body. Kill her! Kill her! Kill her! I won't let them! I won't let them kill me...

Nina noticed a pocket knife attached to the bouncer's belt as they continued their intimate struggle. Out of sheer desperation and in a state of madness, she managed to unsnap the holder and pull the knife from its sheath. As she did, both of them fell to the ground in the slick wetness, tumbling over each other, vying for the top position of control.

"Stop it, Nina. What the fuck's a matter with you? It's me, Ron. You *know* me," he shouted at her during the tumble.

See? See? This monster wants me; it wants to fuck me and then devour my flesh.

"Nina, Jesus! What the hell has gotten into you!?"

I won't let you! I won't let you feed off my body, you hideous thing. You're insane! You are all insane! I'd rather die than let you fuck me!

Nina pulled the small blade from the handle. She let go of Ron's shoulders, grasped her left breast and started slicing. Both of them screamed. The men who were only moments ago chanting and cursing at Nina and Ron now yelled in horror.

Someone shouted 'call an ambulance' while others ran out of the strip club. She began cutting into her right breast just as Ron hit the stage, unconscious from shock.

Donald had been in his office. He didn't want to make Nina nervous by having him watching during her first night back at work. Since she was scheduled for a second performance at midnight, he planned to watch then, from his special place behind the bar. But over the last five minutes, he had listened to a cacophony that was not in keeping with a regular audience watching a stripper. When he heard someone call for an ambulance, he had to see what was happening on the main floor.

Donald practically flew down the hallway to the open room. For a split second he stood motionless, trying to make sense of all the chaos. People were running and screaming, furniture had been tipped over, glasses were shattered, music still blared through the speakers, strobe lights continued to flash. A couple of guys were throwing up in one of the corners by the bathrooms.

Blood. His eyes locked onto the blood. He ran toward the stage, seeing Ron first, passed out in the midst of a water-logged mess. He appeared to have a small cut on his head. Donald still didn't understand the reason for the mêlée, until he looked over to the far left and saw his bartender hunched over someone.

Nina.

"Holy shit! What happened?" Bickley choked out, not yet seeing the full extent of her injuries. When he stepped over to her, he saw...

"It…it all happened so fast, Mr. Bickley. I'm not even sure what *did* happen up here…," the bartender said, half dazed.

"Go…go call 9-1-1. I'll stay with her," Bickley whispered. His eyes never left her face. "Nina? Nina, dear, it's me, Donald. Can you hear me?"

She mumbled, still holding the knife. She was losing blood quickly. Her eyes connected with Donald's and she forced a partial smile.

"I know you…you're not a monster."

"There's an ambulance on the way; you just hold on a little bit longer, okay? Can you do that?"

"Uh hunh…"

"Can…can you tell me who did this to you? Was it someone here?"

"Uh uh…n-nuh…"

"Hold on there, my dear. You hold on. Help is on the way."

"Monster… mons…"

"Who? Who's a monster? Who did this to you? Can you tell me?"

The scream of the sirens vibrated through the building. Flashes of red and blue competed with the strobe lights from the stage. Donald could hear voices outside, orders being given, equipment being taken off of vehicles. Donald bent down and whispered in her ear.

"Nina, who was it? *Who did this to you?*"

Then, to block out all the other noise, he laid his ear against her lips.

"Karl."

CHAPTER 30

KARL'S FINAL MEETING

▲ ▲ ▲

"THANKS FOR COMING OVER HERE on such short notice, Wegan. Things have been a little dicey around the Finchon, so I thought the Lounge would be a better place to meet."

"Not a problem either way, man. I'm just glad we're finally doing business together."

"Come on back," Karl said, ushering Wegan into his office and closing the door behind them.

"Something to drink? I can have Tracy whip up anything you want."

"No, I'm good."

"Okay, down to business. I like that."

"Let me ask you first. What happened to your other supplier? I thought you were happy with the guy an' that's why I wasn't hearing from you."

"Well, yeah, I was...for a while. But, you know how it is in this game. People change. Other opportunities come along. So, you know, long story short, he's out and you're in."

While Karl and Wegan discussed the finer points of trafficking drugs into Badfish, Donald Bickley was having his own serious conversation with an EMT. As Nina was being loaded up into the ambulance for St. Ignatius hospital in Coral Creek, it was very difficult for the medical professionals to hide their grim expression from Donald as they strapped her onto the stretcher.

He asked if she would be okay, if she was going to make it. He assured them that money wasn't an issue and that they should do whatever was needed in order to keep her alive. The driver took him aside, privately sharing a medical opinion that shouldn't have been shared with someone who was not family. Donald swallowed hard and held back tears as the driver gave him a hug and a solid pat on the back before getting behind the wheel. He didn't move a muscle until the ambulance was completely out of sight.

Around 10:30pm, Donald stopped at a gas station/convenience store before heading over to the Finchon. When Neil told him that he hadn't seen his boss all day, and that he was probably over at the Lionfish Lounge, Donald handed him a hundred dollar bill and told him not to let his boss know that he had stopped by.

He turned the key and the engine roared. Slamming his foot on the gas, seat belt squashed beneath the weight of his body, Donald drove directly to the Lionfish. His tires squealed as he drove from the street into the parking lot, nearly spinning out of control, but slowed once the rubber hit the gravel. He stopped and counted: one, two, three, four, five cars. One was Karl's, one was Tracy's, one was the evening kitchen help, and one had to be the cook. That left one uncertainty – another worker or perhaps a customer. It really didn't matter either way, because in Donald's mind, this was going to happen.

He pulled a handgun out of a brown paper bag and tucked it into his coat pocket. He got out of his car and went into the Lounge. Instantly, he knew. The extra car must belong to another worker since the place was empty. He walked up to Tracy, who was sitting behind the bar reading a book.

"Is your boss here?"

"Oh, hi, Mr. Bickley. Yeah, he's been here for about an hour but he's in a meeting right now. Do you want me to let him know that you're here?"

"No, no need for that. I'll just wait until he's done. Can I get a beer?"

"Sure. What would you like?"

"How about something with a kick to it? You got anything like that back there?"

"Uh…yeah, actually I do. I think we got this by accident. It's Chipotle beer. See, the bottle says 'beer with a kick'. If you end up hating it, just let me know. I won't charge you for it."

Tracy opened the bottle and set it in front of Donald with an ice cold glass next to it.

"Don't need a glass."

"Drinkin' it straight, huh?" she laughed, hoping to break the intensity of his mood.

"Yep. Straight."

Donald turned and sat at a table facing one of the corner televisions, his back to the hallway and Karl's office. Tracy paused for a beat, then two. She knew by now that some people just didn't want to make small talk and that was fine with her.

She sat on the stool behind the bar and continued to read her paperback.

Twenty minutes went by before Donald asked for another drink. He had no idea who Karl was meeting with, but he could wait. He had all the time in the world.

He was finishing his second beer just as he heard voices from down the hallway; two men talking quietly. The tone sounded friendly, yet businesslike. Donald stayed put with his back to them, listening.

"I appreciate you coming over and I'm glad we could connect on those issues," Karl said.

"It's not a problem. I'll email you with the specifics by this weekend, okay?"

"Perfect. Hey, you want a drink before you take off? Tracy'll make anything you want. She's the best bartender in Badfish, aren't you?" Karl winked at Tracy, an action that made her stomach turn.

"That's okay. I gotta take off. No offense, Tracy. Maybe next time."

Wegan waved and walked out the door as Karl stood there, gazing at nothing in particular.

"Uh, Karl? There's a man over there that's been waiting to see you. I don't know what it's about, but he's been here quite a while."

"Who, that guy? Oh." Karl nodded and smiled as recognition washed over his face. "Yeah, I know that guy. What the hell's that fuckin' faggot want to see me for?"

"I told him that you were tied up in a meeting, but he said he was going to wait for you no matter how long it took. He hasn't said anything to me except to order a couple of beers."

"Alright. I'll handle it."

Karl walked over to Donald. Donald stood to meet him, eye to eye.

"Bickley, what brings you to my neck of the woods? Tracy says you've been waiting for a while."

"I have."

"I got no business with you, Donald. Why the fuck are you in my lounge? I'm not runnin' a damn gay bar here."

"We need to talk. Right now."

"*We* don't need to do a fuckin' thing. If you're so hopped up to talk to me, why can't you pick up a phone? I don't want to see your ugly mug around here scarin' away my customers."

"From the looks of things, it don't seem to me like you got many to scare away."

"What do you want? Just tell me and get the hell out of here."

"I think it would be best if we talked in private."

"Fine," Karl sighed. "Tracy, if I'm not out of my office in fifteen minutes, knock on my door and make sure Bickley isn't on top of me raping my ass."

Tracy looked up from her book without a single word.

Both men walked wordlessly down the hall and into Karl's office. Donald sat in the chair directly in front of Karl's desk and Karl took his own seat, facing Bickley. More than a moment of silent tension passed, enough that it could be hacked off with a scythe; and though both men sensed it, neither felt compelled to begin the dialogue. Finally, Karl broke.

"So. Donald Bickley. I guess Badfish isn't as small as everyone thinks it is 'cause I haven't seen you for quite some time."

"Don't think we travel in the same circles, is all."

"No, I suppose we don't. You got me there. So, tell me, how are your brothers doing?"

"Don't talk to 'em."

"Can't imagine why."

"Fuck off, Karl."

"Why are you here, Donald? Screw all these pleasantries 'cause they're not all that pleasant."

"Nina. Do you know her?"

"Who are you talking about?"

Donald adjusted himself in his seat.

"I want to know if you know a dancer named Nina Dumont."

"Maybe. What business is it of yours?"

"Nina *is* my business. I'm her boss and I want to know if you know her, and if you do, how *well* do you know her?"

"You know, that's really none of your business. But, I'm in a good mood tonight because I just had a very productive meeting that's going to make me a lot of money. So, I'm going to play this game of yours. But first, let me clue you in to the fact that Nina is way the hell out of your age bracket. See, at *my* age, I can squeak by, but you? That would be worse than pathetic; it would just be sad. And second? I probably know a hell of a lot more about her than you do. Sure, she might work for you. Hell, she might even give you private pussy dances after everyone else leaves and it's just the two of you in your office. But I see her every fuckin' day. I know her better than you ever will, and that's because she lives at the Finchon."

"No. That's a lie."

"No, Bickley. That's a *truth* and has been for some time now. I can prove it if you really need to see it in writing. I've got signed contracts. She's even paid up through February. So, if you want her to move in with you or some shit like that, you can tell her that she's about to lose two months of rent money."

"She lives in an apartment near Coral Creek. New apartments near the edge of town."

"Sorry to break it to ya, pal, but you're talking about Nina the stripper, right? The one with the long hair who wears the slinky costumes and is *this* tall and weighs about 105 pounds soaking wet? If that's the one you mean, then *you're the one* who's been lied to. That chick lives alone in Room 301 and has for some time now. So…I don't know what story she's laying on you, but…"

Donald's face turned a fierce shade of red. Karl couldn't tell if he was angry or embarrassed or both.

"This isn't making sense…she told me…"

"She probably also mentioned that we've been seeing each other."

Donald stood up, launching his chair backwards into the couch. Target hit, it toppled over on its side and lay like a helpless victim.

"No! Now you *are* lying, you asshole. She isn't seeing anyone. She would have told me."

"Hey," Karl rose up slowly. "I don't know what's going on between you guys, but Nina and I *have* been together for some time now. Actually, we hooked up as soon as she moved in. But sadly, we broke it off yesterday. She's a free agent...at least she was when I left her place last night."

"You were with her last night?"

"If you must pry, yes, I was with her. I took her out to dinner. And that's the only detail you're getting, Bickley. You and your twisted mind will just have to come up with whatever mental image you're looking for on your own. You *do* realize that she can make up her own mind about who to go out with...and who *not* to..."

"What about drugs? That dump you run over there is teeming with that filth. Could she have gotten into something like that?"

"Hey, look who's talking about running a shithole."

"Don't call Bickley's a shithole. It might be a strip club, but it's still ten times classier than that dive you own. Place can't even pass for a no-tell motel anymore. Just a hole for the scum of the earth to wallow in, and you're pathetic enough to charge 'em rent to stay there."

"Uh, *Nina* is staying there. Are you lumping your wet dream girlfriend in with the rest of the scum, as you call them? "

"You must have tricked her. I don't know what you said to that poor girl, but you must have run some damn con to get her to stay in a place like that. It had to be drugs...it just had to be."

Karl sat back down, hoping Donald would follow suit. He did, but not immediately.

"*What* had to be drugs?"

Donald hesitated. He wasn't sure how much information he was ready to share, especially since he didn't know what really happened. He made a mental note to call the hospital when he was done with Karl before driving over there again. He wanted desperately to hang on to a shred of hope.

"They took Nina to the hospital this evening."

"They? Who's they?"

"The ambulance. They were called to the club. She was in bad shape when they got there. Real bad."

"No shit? What the hell happened?"

"I don't know. By the time I got out to the stage, everything was a damn nightmare already. Guys running everywhere, my bouncer was passed out, tables and chairs all over the place. It looked like a war zone and all that was left was the dead and dying."

"What about Nina?"

"*I told you*; she was in pretty bad shape. That's why I think drugs had a part in all this."

"Why? Did she say something?"

"As a matter of fact, she did."

Karl started to sweat. He knew that if Donald suspected him, even in the slightest, things could turn ugly in a heartbeat. He yanked a couple Kleenexes from the box off his desk and wiped his forehead.

"You nervous 'bout something, Karl? It's the middle of December and you're sweating. Should I be asking some other kinds of questions here?"

"Uh, no. No, not at all. I'm just upset about Nina. You come in here telling me this story about her being hurt, taking drugs... you know. I-I just saw her last night. I told you, the dinner, the wine..."

"I don't recall you mentioning wine. Was she drunk? I just assumed this had something to do with drugs. What the fuck aren't you telling me, Karl?"

"No, uh...well, maybe she had wine with dinner, come to think of it. I...uh, shoot. I don't remember what we ordered... maybe *I* had the wine..."

Donald stood up and leaned across the desk. Compared to Karl's diminutive stature, Donald was overwhelming. The overture made him sweat even more. He looked at Bickley's hands, fisted balls of anger, and realized this guy must out-weigh him by at least seventy-five pounds. A physical fight would not end well for him. His mind flashed to an image of him sharing a hospital room with Nina, thinking that he might end up there tonight anyway depending on how he answered Donald's questions.

"Sounds like you have something to tell me, Karl." He leaned in more, closing the gap between their faces. "I suggest you start from the beginning. And if I don't like what I hear, there's going to be trouble."

"I told you the truth, Bickley. And I'm sure as hell not go-ing to be threatened in my own office. I think it might be time for you to leave."

"I'm not leaving until I hear what went on between the two of you, because something tells me that what happened *today* is connected to something that happened *last night*."

Karl stood up, drenched in his own sweat.

"Get out, you faggot. *Now.* Or I'll call the cops."

Donald stood up and straightened his coat. He noticed the phone on the desk but it didn't faze him. He reached into his coat pocket very slowly and pulled out a Smith & Wesson. He pointed it square at Karl's head and sat back down in the chair. Karl's mouth dropped open as his hands went up.

"No, I don't think you'll be calling anybody. What I do think is that you're going to sit back down in your chair, place your hands on your head where I can see them, and tell me exactly what happened between you and Nina."

"I told you, Bickley. Please. Please put the gun away. This whole thing is getting way out of hand."

"Start talking."

"Okay, okay," Karl shrugged and cringed a little. "Uh, let's see. I went over to her room, we exchanged pleasantries and I drove to the restaurant."

"Go on."

"Well, um, then we ordered and ate. It doesn't sound exciting, but that's what happened. There's a waiter at the restaurant who would tell you the exact same thing."

"Did she drink anything during dinner?"

"Uh, I don't recall...yes?"

"Continue."

"Okay...uh, dinner, dessert. Then, she drove us back to the motel."

"Why did *she* drive?"

"Because maybe *I* had a few too many. You never asked if I had anything to drink, did you?"

"That's because I don't give a rat's ass about *you*. Keep going…she drove you home, then what?"

"Then I said that I had an early Christmas present for her and that I would get it and be right back. And that's exactly what I did. I went to my office, grabbed the bag and went back to her room. She was dressed; all the lights were on, everything was completely normal. I swear. You can ask her for yourself; that's exactly what happened. Can you at least lower the gun, Bickley?"

"It's fine where it is. What did you give her?"

"Wine. A very expensive bottle of pinot. And, yes, before you ask, we *both* drank from the bottle."

"How was she when you left?"

"The same as when I got there. Fine."

Donald scratched his head with his free hand. Something didn't add up. Why would she say Karl was responsible? There was a piece missing. He put the gun back in his coat pocket and stood.

"I don't ever want to see you around Nina again, you hear me?"

"That's not your decision to make."

"Tonight it is," he said, patting his coat pocket. He turned around and left the office, leaving Karl to sweat it out alone.

CHAPTER 31

CODE BLUE

▲ ▲ ▲

DONALD PRACTICALLY RAN DOWN THE hallway of St. Ignatius's emergency wing. He wasn't familiar with the building at all, having been in it only one other time: the day his dad had a fatal stroke some thirty odd years ago. It was one of his favorite memories.

Donald and his two brothers had been waiting for hours in the visitor's room. The odd hospital lighting reflected off the lime-green paint and cast eerie shadows behind each of the three men. They were anxious to know what could have caused an old steady farmer like their father, who had been working up until that very afternoon in the fields, to fall off his tractor without warning. The oldest brother, Paul, had actually carried their dad to the pick-up before driving him to the ER. When the doctors and nurses took over, Paul took the opportunity to call Donald and their brother, Delbert, from the pay phone in the lobby.

The trio sat there, frustrated. Delbert and Paul, sitting side by side on faux leather chairs, made a feeble attempt at some idle chit chat, but both men knew it was only to pass the time. With farms and families of their own, they only spoke to each other a few times a year; birthdays and Christmas.

Donald stood on the other side of the room, thumbing through old, crinkled magazines full of expired coupons. He was there only out of family obligation, and if he could manage getting through this nightmare of a day without so much as making eye contact with his brothers, so much the better.

A doctor, donned in light green scrubs, pulled the double doors wide open and stepped into the visitor's room. His mask hung down and dangled comically under his chin like a miniature hammock.

"Bickley? Paul Bickley?"

Paul and Delbert stood at the same time.

"Yes, that's me. This is my brother, Delbert. How's our dad?"

The doctor eyed Donald from across the room.

"Why don't we go talk in a more private setting," the doctor said. "That way, we can speak freely without bothering anyone else waiting for news about *their* family."

"Oh. That's our brother. Donald."

"Do you think he might want to join us then?"

Paul snapped his fingers to get Donald's attention, but he was already on his way. He was not about to miss any news regarding his dad's health.

"Doctor," he said, holding out his hand. Paul and Delbert exchanged eye rolls.

"Yes, good to meet you, Donald. Why don't we go in here and talk."

The four men entered a very small conference cubicle just off the main waiting room. Everyone squeezed in, forcing a physical closeness that was barely tolerable.

"Okay, this is where we're at. Your father's had a major stroke. We call it a hemorrhagic stroke because when the aneurysm ruptures, it causes severe bleeding, *hemorrhaging*, if you will. By the time we got to him in the ER, there really wasn't anything that we could do. Unfortunately, in about ten percent of these kinds of strokes, the outcome is fairly immediate. I'm really very sorry, but when this type of aneurysm occurs, there is no recourse. I *can* tell you that it was quick."

Paul and Delbert grasped each other's shoulders as their tears fell. Delbert pulled a handkerchief out of his back pocket and blew his nose while Paul covered his face with his free hand. Donald's eyes widened.

"Tell me, Doctor. Did he suffer at all? Could you tell?"

"Donald, I really can't say for sure, but if I was being honest, sometimes the person can have immense pain in their head. Sort of like the worst headache they've ever had in their life. In your father's case, it's impossible to say because he had already passed when we got to him."

"Thank you, Doctor." Donald said. He squeezed passed his brothers, opened the door and walked out. He practically waltzed down the hallway and out of the hospital, smiling and free.

In regard to Nina, the situation was very different. The *last* thing he wanted was for her to be in any kind of pain: physical, mental or emotional. He scanned the area for the Admitting Desk.

"Excuse me; I'm looking for Nina Dumont. I believe she was brought in a few hours ago."

"Are you related to her?"

"Yes. I'm her uncle," Donald lied.

"She was taken to Room 18. Just over there, around the corner."

"Thank you."

He approached the Emergency Room partition with trepidation; feelings of anxiousness and dread welled up inside him as he thought about what might be waiting on the other side. A nurse came up behind him holding a bed pan.

"Excuse me, sir. Are you coming in here?"

"Oh, yeah. Guess I don't like hospitals very much. No offense of course."

"We get that a lot around here, so, no I'm not offended. I don't think anyone likes these places too much, especially the patients."

Donald nodded. He was certain that Nina didn't like being here.

When he walked in and saw her lying on the bed with tubes and IV's protruding from her, he felt nauseous. A surgical procedure had already been done because he saw bandages and wrapping over her chest and torso. He stood over the bed and whispered her name, hoping she would respond to his voice. A part of him realized that she wouldn't answer; they must have loaded her up with enough drugs to knock her out for quite a while. A doctor walked in, clipboard in hand.

"Hello."

"Hi, I'm Doctor Tobias. I was the doctor on call when Miss Dumont was brought into the ER. And you are...?"

"Donald Bickley, her uncle. I live over in Badfish."

"Okay, Donald. Can you tell me anything about Nina's past twenty-four hours?"

"What do you mean?"

"I mean, what did she take? What kind of drugs was she on? We've run a number of blood tests and while some of them came back fine, as they should for someone of her age and stature, there were some pretty alarming toxicity results."

"Drugs? Nina doesn't do drugs. I would've known about that."

"I'm sorry to have to be the one to tell you, but your niece's system is teeming with some kind of compound that I've never seen before. It's a combination of codeine and some extremely hazardous materials. Come to think of it, this reminds me of Krokadil. You ever hear of it?"

"What's Krokadil?"

"Well, the medical name is Desomorphine. Usually, people will make it themselves by cooking codeine and adding paint thinner or gasoline. Sometimes they add hydrochloric acid or iodine or even the red phosphorous from matchbox strike pads. Then, if you can believe it, they inject this liquid right into their veins in order to get some kind of super high."

"Oh, my God. What the hell are they thinking, putting that kind of garbage into themselves?"

"From what I've read, these people think they're making heroin, but believe me, this is a thousand times worse. I've seen some of the pictures, Mr. Bickley. The end result can be pretty gruesome. We're talking bones protruding out of arms and legs. In some cases, a person's skin will be completely eaten away or turn black and peel off. It's actually the most horrific thing I've ever seen, and I've been in the medical field for about eleven years."

"And you're telling me this is what Nina took? This *Krokadil?*"

"No, we don't think it's Krokadil in her system, but the way she cut herself and her emotional outbursts when she was first brought in are very similar to someone having taken it. Plus, our initial toxicity results showed some very questionable chemicals floating through her bloodstream."

"Is it possible she could have taken this…this *thing* without knowing it?"

"Like a spiked drink? A date rape drug? Sure, it's possible. I mean, even something as common as aspirin; every person will have a different reaction to it. Why don't we wait until more test results come in, alright? In the meantime, if you can think of anything she might have taken or come across, let us know right away."

"Of course. Anything to help her."

"Good. I can see your niece means quite a lot to you, Donald. We'll do everything we can for her."

While Donald waited for the rest of the lab results, he headed downstairs to the cafeteria. Hunger wasn't necessarily his motivation, but it was something to do to fill the time. He settled for a ham salad sandwich, plain chips and a Pepsi. The cashier rang it up: $10.85. He shot her a disgusted look and handed her a twenty.

"Highway robbery," he muttered.

"I just work here, sir. I don't make the prices. Have a nice day."

Donald grumbled, pocketed the change and found a quiet table in a far corner. A section of newspaper left behind by a previous patron lay on the corner of the table. He opened it up to an article about the latest trends on decorating the home for Christmas *just like the good old days*. Between bites, he found himself gazing around the hospital lobby, watching people come and go rather than reading up on holidays of yore. He took another bite of his sandwich when he looked at the entryway and nearly choked.

Karl.

What the hell was he doing here?

Donald quickly picked up what was left of the meal and tossed it in the closest garbage can. As stealthily as he could, he followed him to the ER, hanging back and listening as Karl explained to the Admitting Desk that he was Nina's uncle who just got the word that she had been brought in. Once they allowed him past security, Donald trailed far enough behind and stood on the outside of the curtain while Karl went in and sat beside Nina's bed.

"Nina? Can you hear me? It's Karl. Look, I'm hopin' that you *can* hear me. I don't know what happened at Bickley's, but I guess you're in pretty bad shape, huh? Uh, I just want you to know that *I'm* not going to say anything, okay? I mean, you can't tell anybody either, alright? You know, about the wine? Please, just don't tell them or the cops about that. God. *Fuck.* I-I was so pissed off at your attitude; I dumped the whole thing of 'orange' in the wine. I've been giving you a little bit here an' there. It was fun, wasn't it? I didn't know you'd react like this. Aren't you s'posed to build up some kind of tolerance or something like that? Shit, I didn't know. Yeah, okay. *Maybe I did.* I fucked up. I just came by to…I don't know…say sorry… or…something."

Donald heard Karl getting up from the chair, so he ducked around a corner near the nurses' station. Peering out from around the corner, he watched Karl part the curtain and walk out, giving a quick wave to a passing nurse. Donald waited until he felt enough time had passed for Karl to have left the building before he took the nearest exit down the stairs and out to the parking lot. From a thoughtful distance, he followed Karl back to the Finchon.

Meanwhile, one of the nurses on duty went to check vitals on Nina. The numbers were way off and she was unresponsive.

"Code Blue, Room 18!"

A medical team rushed in to do everything they could, but this time it wasn't enough. The cuts were bad - deep and violent, having ripped through chest muscle tissue, and she had lost a lot of blood in the process. Over the past few hours, many of her organs had battled to stay aloft, but were now losing their fight. However, it wasn't the massive blood loss that ended Nina's existence. *That* came solely from Karl's drugs.

CHAPTER 32

THE FINCHON MOTEL

▲ ▲ ▲

A FEW MINUTES BEFORE MIDNIGHT, Karl sped into the parking lot, jumped out of his car and ran into the office. Neil looked up from his cell phone long enough to see a blur of his boss run past him without so much as a nod of acknowledgment. The office door slammed shut, leaving Neil to stare slack-jawed at nothing and no one. He shrugged it off and continued playing Candy Crush Saga, having missed the next level by one wrapped candy.

Minutes later, Donald pulled into the motel's parking lot from the other side where the view of the main office window was obscured by a post. He killed his headlights, turned off the ignition and sat quietly in the dark, waiting. Dozens of scenarios played out in his mind, some better than others, and some *more likely* than others. He ran each possibility through his head, weighing the positives against the negatives before deciding which one to put into action.

A sharp knock on the driver's side window startled him out of his contemplation. He looked out and saw a skinny black man wearing clothes far too large for his thin frame. The man made a motion for Donald to roll down his window. He hesitated for a moment but gave in and lowered it slightly.

"What?"

"How you doin' tonight? Can I interest you in something special on an evening as fine as this one?

"If you think I'm sitting here waiting to buy drugs, you better think again. Why don't you go bother someone else?"

"A'ight. Take it easy, man. I'm just asking you a question. Businessman to businessman. But that's fine. I'll be on my way," G-Force said as he tipped his hat to Donald.

"Wait. Wait a second. Do you live here in the motel?"

"I surely do. Why do you ask?"

"Can I ask you some questions?"

"Depends. Are you the law?"

"Not hardly."

"How do I know that?"

"Well, let's see. You just offered me drugs and I didn't bust your ass, so, that's one. And two, have you ever been to Bickley's strip club?"

"Oh, yeah. Mighty fine women there. We have a few of them living right here. Whoever owns that place is the luckiest man alive. He's set for life, you dig?"

"Well, I'm him. I'm Donald Bickley, the owner."

G-Force stepped back and took an overly dramatic look at him through the crack in the window.

"You're shittin' me."

"I am not shitting you in the least," Donald said, removing his wallet and flipping it open to show the man his driver's license.

"Well, I'll be. I'm in the presence of greatness. You've got some damn fine women working for you. You're one lucky son-of-a-bitch."

"I'd like to ask you some questions. Can I do that?"

G-Force shivered, rubbed his hands together and blew on them with his hot breath.

"That'd be fine, Mr. B., but if it's all the same to you, I rather talk somewhere warm."

"Hop in," Donald said. He reached over and unlocked the passenger door.

▲ ▲ ▲

"So, let me get this straight. Karl, the owner of this place, supplies you with the drugs and then you and your people sell 'em and you all split the money?"

"Yeah, that's pretty much it. I mean, he gets most of it of course, but we do okay."

"Is there a certain kind of drug he gives you, or does it vary?"

"*Very?*"

"Change. You know, one week, cocaine, the next week, pot. That type of thing."

G-Force laughed hard enough to wipe a tear from the corner of his eye.

"*Pot?* Where have you been, Mr. B., 1975? Shit, you're funny. No, it's nothing like that anymore. What he gives us is special.

I guarantee you've never seen anything like it. Not now or back in your day."

"What's so special about it? It costs more? Harder to get? What?"

G-Force carefully opened his coat and pulled a loaded syringe out of a side pocket. He held it gingerly, beaming with pride to be able to introduce the product to someone new.

"This is what's so special. It's called 'orange'. It will fuck you up big time. Worse than any other drug. This stuff is evil shit, Mr. B."

"If it's so bad, why the hell do you sell it to people?"

"Same reason the boss gives it to us: money."

"Can this stuff kill someone?"

"Hell, Mr. B., I've seen it do a lot worse than that. Sure, a person might die from it, but what happens *before* they die…oh, shit. Nasty-ass stuff, man. Nasty."

"Do you know if anyone *here* was into it? You know, someone living at the motel?"

G shrugged. "Can't say for sure, but, yeah, I'd bet there's some going around."

"One more question. Do you know if Karl was seeing anyone, you know, dating someone from the Finchon?"

"Oh, yeah. I don't know what he's got, but damn if he wasn't seeing this one hotty," he giggled incessantly. "She was in 301, right next to my man, Bobby. Shit, Bobby works at your club. Huh, you know, I haven't seen that boy in a while…but, that's one thing you can count on around here. People are here one minute and then…poof."

Donald sat silently for a minute, letting everything sink in. Room 301. It had to be Nina's room.

"Okay, can I ask you one more question?"

"Shoot."

"Can you get me into that room? Room 301?"

"You want me to break in? I dunno about that."

"I'll pay you," Donald added, taking his wallet out again. He held up a hundred dollar bill.

"Okay," G smiled. His eyes grew wide; he nodded in time, as if listening to a tuneful song. "I'll get you into any room you want. You keep those coming and I'll bring you room service myself."

▲ ▲ ▲

With some sleight of hand from a borrowed credit card, G-Force and Donald found themselves standing in the middle of Nina's motel room. Clothes had been strewn about: sweatshirts, pants, a thong, parts of a dance costume. The bed was a mess and there were a few towels on the floor, but nothing jumped out to either man as being out of the ordinary. They walked together into the bathroom, and found it in the same condition: hairbrush, make-up, spilled powder, toothbrush. Again, nothing unusual.

"Well, let me do a little more digging around here on my own, okay? I appreciate everything. You've been most helpful," Donald said, handing over the large bill. He added another $20. "Here, for keeping all of this between you and me."

"Not a peep, Mr. B. Not a single peep," G said, exchanging a modified handshake with Donald. He pressed a finger to his lips, as if to shush himself and scurried out the door, closing it quietly from the outside.

Donald placed his hands on his hips and scanned the area. He wanted to find some kind of incriminating evidence against Karl, something concrete aside from what he overheard at the hospital. He also had a compelling desire to lie on Nina's bed and bury himself under her clothes and underwear.

One thing was certain; this *was* Nina's room. She lived here alone - no roommates, no high rent bill, and no fancy new apartment on the other side of town.

Why did she lie to me? I gave her plenty of money so she wouldn't have to live in such squalor. Karl. He must have brainwashed her — that could be the only reason for her to agree to live in such a place. That motherfucker took everything from her and then had the gall to show up at the hospital.

Donald's eyes fell upon a silky tie from one of Nina's costumes. He leaned across the bed and put it to his nose, taking in as much of her scent as he could. He rubbed it against his lips and across his eyes, aching to be near her. Although he knew that seeing her again was impossible, he couldn't help but long for her unrequited love.

Donald gathered up a few personal items from the room, turned the lights out, shut the door and went to his car. He placed the items inside the trunk before heading to the main office.

Karl was tossing papers and files everywhere in a hasty attempt to collect anything that could incriminate him with regard to Nina, in case she decided to talk to the authorities. He came across a few sex charged correspondences, complete with heart shapes dotting the i's and smiley faces near her signature, but he thought there were more. He uncovered receipts - some for the SeaGrass and some for other expensive restaurants. He found others for jewelry and shoes, lists of items to look for the next time he was in the city, doodles of her name, including sex acts and profanity. He stopped in mid-search the moment he heard voices coming from the main office. He froze, straining to hear.

"Where's Karl?"

"Good evening, sir and welcome to the Finchon. We are happy to have you here. How can I help you?" Neil stated robotically as he read from a paper on the counter.

"Where's your boss?"

"Perhaps *I* can be of service to you. What may I do for you?" Neil continued reading.

Donald ripped the paper from Neil's hands. He crumpled it up and threw it in the corner.

"Kid, I'm not interested in your script. Where's Karl? In his office?

"Yes, sir. Right in there," Neil hitched his thumb back toward the closed door. "If you want to wait here for a second, I'll see if he's busy."

"No. He'll see me whether he's busy or not," Donald said as he walked around the customer service counter.

"Uh, you can't just go in…," he started to say, but Donald was already at the threshold of Karl's office. He tried turning the knob but it was locked. He pounded on the door. Karl was pressed up against the back of the door, ear to the wood, trying to get every word.

"Karl, this is Donald Bickley. I know you're in there. Open up."

"No, Bickley. We're done. I don't have anything else to say to you. We finished our business at the Lounge. Neil? Neil, are you out there? Why don't you escort Mr. Bickley to his car?"

"Uh, I don't think he's ready to go, man. He seems pretty set on seeing you."

"Karl, open up *now*. Don't make me break this fuckin' door down."

There was a tiny click, a pause, then another click. The door opened about an inch. Donald pushed it open the rest of the way. He saw Karl seated behind his desk. One hand was on the land line phone and one hand looked to be resting in a side drawer. He was sweating and red-faced; his shirt was wrinkled and his hair was messed up from having run his hands through it.

Donald glanced back into the main office and whispered to Neil.

"Why don't you go outside for awhile? We'll be okay in here."

"You sure? I don't wanna get the boss pissed off at me for leaving the counter."

"I promise. You'll be fine."

Neil shrugged and grabbed his jacket off the coat rack. He took another look at Bickley and walked out. Donald closed the office door. He stood facing Karl, neither man wanting to make the first move.

"Bickley, I don't know what you're doing here, but I don't think we have anything else to say to each other. You can either get the fuck out of here, you faggot, or I'm calling the cops."

"I know it was you, Karl. You gave Nina the drugs."

"I-I don't know what the hell you're talking about, but you have about ten seconds to leave. One…two…three…"

"You'll never make ten, you motherfucker," Donald said.

Within the span of three seconds, before Karl had a chance to react, Donald pulled his weapon, aimed it at Karl and shot him right between the eyes. If there was one thing Donald Bickley had learned to do well while growing up on the farm, it was sharp-shooting on a dime. While he wasn't able to defend himself against his father or brothers, he could shoot the hell out of any target put in front of him.

Karl never knew what hit him. It happened so quickly, he never saw Bickley pull the gun from his pocket. The bullet had less than eight feet to travel, so when it hit him, it was immediate. He was alive one minute and dead the next. No ambiguity and no purgatory. The hole, dead center between his eyes, looked comically like a third eye up until a red stream of blood broke open and ran down his face. The velocity of the shot knocked him back against his chair, putting him in a relaxed position, as if he had worked a long, hard day and was taking a breather.

Donald spit at Karl's body and turned to leave. He paused at the doorway right before he walked out.

"You fucked with Nina. Nobody fucks with Nina."

CHAPTER 33

THE AFTERMATH

▲ ▲ ▲

FOUR LARGE "FOR SALE" SIGNS, complete with a realtor's name and cell number, stood at attention along the main driveway that led up to the Finchon motel. Everyone who had been living there, whether they were staying a couple nights or regulars who had been there for years had been questioned. They were either let go or were transferred to the county shelter during the days and weeks that followed the murder of Karl Demetris. When the county police came in and swept the buildings, they uncovered more drugs and paraphernalia during that operation than they had found over the past three years from five other drug stings.

A few people were taken into custody for selling or possession, but G-Force managed to walk away unscathed. He quietly moved to the next town over and shacked up with one of those *fine women* that worked at Bickley's. When the police had searched his room, they found nothing except some empty cheese and cracker wrappers from the gas station's vending machine.

When the police questioned Neil, he told them that he went out for a break and when he got back to the office thirty minutes later, everything was quiet. He finished his shift and went home. He admitted that he never looked in Karl's office because he had always been told that 'unless something was on fire, the boss was not to be disturbed.' He never mentioned a word about Donald's visit on the night in question.

Donald Bickley told the police everything he knew - how Karl had used the Finchon as a hub for drug running, illegal activity and possible prostitution. He explained how badly Karl had treated his staff and how he *alone* was responsible for bringing the deadly drug into the area, which ultimately led to the death of Nina Dumont and possibly others.

Donald suggested that the motel be burned to the ground and completely rebuilt or at least gutted so someone could start over from the beginning. Within a week, a real estate company took hold of the property and set a price.

Now that Karl was truly gone, Badfish had the opportunity for a clean start. Donald decided to use some of his money to rennovate Bickley's. He put in a new stage, hired experienced bouncers, upgraded the lights and floors, put in a new sound system and upgraded the dressing room. A plaque with Nina's picture hung in the hallway next to his office. Underneath was a silver plate engraved with the years she had worked there. Every time he passed by it, he would touch it and put his hand to his heart.

Tracy tried to keep the Lionfish Lounge afloat but without Karl's financial backing, the bills piled up with no relief in sight. She knew enough about the day-to-day operations and how to manage employees, but the cash simply wasn't there. She was able to keep her head above water for a few weeks but realized that the end was near. After talking with the other employees, they all agreed to close the bar after the next pay period. A few days before they closed, Donald Bickley paid Tracy a visit.

"Mr. Bickley, how are you doing these days? Veronica tells me you've made a lot of changes to your place."

"Yes, I did. It was…well, it was way past time…"

"She says the whole place feels a lot classier now," Tracy added, then started to giggle, "for a strip club."

"Yeah, I know what you mean," Donald nodded. "Shoulda done it a long time ago. I'll kick myself for a long time for not having done it back then, but…well, look, Tracy, I came by because I wanted to talk to *you*."

"Sure," she said as she gestured toward a seat at the end of the bar.

"I'll get right to the point, an' you can tell me to go fuck off if I'm outta line. But, I imagine you're having a hard time making a go of things here without Karl. Or rather, without his *money*."

"Yeah, exactly. I'm not a bar owner. I didn't sign up for this, as they say. As a matter of fact, the rest of the staff and I are planning on closing down in a couple of days. We just can't do it. A couple of the guys are moving to Coral Creek after that, but I don't know what I'm gonna do. I'm not even sure I'm going to stick around the area."

"That's what I figured. I've had an idea bouncing around in my head ever since...well, ever since Karl's mysterious departure from Badfish."

"Did you ever hear any details about what happened? I mean, I know he was killed, but I didn't hear much besides that."

Donald shook his head. "No. I never heard much either."

"I know he could be a real asshole at times. That's probably mean of me to say, especially with everything that's happened, but..."

"It's okay. Karl brought all that garbage on himself. What happened to him had nothing to do with you or anybody else. I'm not sorry he's gone, Tracy. As a matter of fact, I think you're probably a lot better off without him around."

"There's just so many unanswered questions. I mean, was it someone from the motel, you know, out for retribution? Was it just a random thing? Him being in the wrong place at the wrong time?"

"I guess we'll never know that now."

They sat in silence for a moment, allowing the chatter of the television drown out the quiet between them. Donald looked around the room, letting their time together fall into a comfort zone. He was never good at simply *being* with another person, but at least he was trying.

"You know, I think I'll take a beer."

"Something a little off the grid?"

"Yeah. Maybe something with a kick to it," he answered and for the first time that he could remember, he smiled.

CHAPTER 34

FISHIN' TRIP

▲ ▲ ▲

LEONARD, PHIL AND THEIR WIVES were heading back to Badfish from having taken a long excursion to the Upper Peninsula of Michigan. It was a fishing trip for the men and a bonding trip for the women who brought along enough knitting and gossip to last until the wee hours of the morning. Originally, the trip was scheduled as an early birthday getaway for Phil and his wife, but over the past month it evolved into a mini-vacation for the four of them.

The men managed to snag enough fish for a few meals, but the rest of the time they ate out at the local restaurants. They didn't mind in the least; they had a wonderful time and took plenty of pictures to send to the kids. Come Christmas, everyone would have plenty of Michigan souvenir gifts to last at least one lifetime, if not two.

During the long ride, the four of them had discussed making one last stop before going back home. While the men were anxious to stretch the vacation out for as long as they could, the women were hesitant. Both ladies were eager to get back to their routines. They were homebodies at heart, and though sleeping in a strange bed was exciting and different, they missed their own beds and their nightly patterns.

Leonard knew what Phil had in mind regarding their final stop before heading home; they had talked the week prior to the trip, during early morning coffee and the casting of fishing lines.

Leonard had pondered over what had happened over the past ten months: quitting his job at the Finchon, Karl's murder, the sale and new purchase of the motel. It was a lot to take in, especially after having worked so close to a man who ended up gunned down in his own office. Leonard spent countless hours in that very room. He remembered some of the things he had seen and it still haunted him at times. There were moments that he wondered - if he had been working there when the shooter came in, would he have been killed too?

Phil explained to Leonard how the place had changed, especially in the past six months. He suggested that they stay there for a night or two, *just to cleanse the pallet*. At first, Leonard wasn't too keen on the idea. He felt that it would bring back too many bad memories, for himself as well as his wife. But Phil pointed out that once he saw all the changes for himself, how positive and upbeat everything was now, the Finchon wouldn't hold the same horrors as before. It could become a place where they could make good memories and have new experiences. Leonard ultimately agreed. All that was left was to convince the wives.

"It'll be a real hoot, dear. Why, I haven't stepped foot in there since...well, you know. Phil says it's a whole different place now, right? Completely gutted and refurbished down to the nails in the walls."

"Ladies, you have my word. I've been inside and I can tell you that you wouldn't even recognize it. You've had to have seen the paper. They even changed the name. That's got to tell you something," Phil laughed.

"Yes, but that doesn't necessarily mean anything. You can whitewash an old barn, but it still stinks when you walk through the door. Leonard, are you telling me that you really want to spend a night there? After everything you've been through?"

"Well, dear, Phil has a point. I think it's high time that we have a *good* experience there. It was such a big part of our lives for so long. Let's try to see it from a different angle."

"Lenore, what do you think? Should we put up with these guys for another night or two, listenin' to them talk about fishing?"

"Well, I suppose we should," she laughed. "I guess I'm curious to see what's become of the place myself. I've heard things, but I've just never made the effort to see it with my own eyes."

"Okay, men, you've convinced us. To the motel, and be quick about it!"

▲ ▲ ▲

Leonard and Phil exited the truck and held the doors open for their wives who were in the back seat chatting up a storm about a recipe of Butternut Squash Pie from the most recent edition of <u>Farm and Country</u>. Apparently, neither of them could get over the fact that the recipe called for a shot of bourbon. That point alone was worth a serious debate.

While the men gathered the luggage from the trunk, the women walked ahead of them, continuing the conversation about whether a pie should dare to have liquor in it or not. Leonard followed Phil up the walk to the main door of the motel and stopped.

"Hey, buddy, are you okay? You know, we don't have to do this if you're not ready," Phil offered.

"I just needed a minute, you know? I didn't think it would hit me so hard, but walking up this old path an' coming up to the doors...I don't know. Kinda tough to get my head around the whole darn thing."

"I understand. Let me go inside and handle everything, okay? You just take as long as you need. And Leonard, if you walk in and decide that now is not the time, I'm with you, okay? We'll leave in a heartbeat," Phil said, putting a hand on his friend's shoulder.

"Thanks. I'll be along. I just need a minute."

Phil nodded, picked up some of the bags and went inside to join the women.

Leonard set his own bags down and looked up. The last time he stood in front of this building, he and Karl had a brutal argument. They fought and Leonard retaliated by quitting; turning in his keys and walking out. He had never quit a job before, but Karl pushed him over the edge. And now Karl was dead, supposedly murdered by a drug addict, according to the county police. But that was almost a year ago, a time when everything in Badfish bordered on chaos - the people, the businesses, and the economy.

These days, the town of Badfish thrived. Once Karl's influence, along with the flow of drugs and corruption had dissipated, people began to see opportunities again. New shops opened and families slowly migrated into the neighborhoods. The Finchon, now known as The Badfish Inn, not only had a brand new highway sign but could boast about having clean, renovated rooms. The pool was sparkling and immaculate with warm towels for each guest. Everything was bright and fresh and welcoming.

Plans were made for small cafes to open just down the block from the Badfish Inn. A group of regional independent artists had been keeping an eye and ear open to all the changes being made. They started making inquiries about setting up shops along the main drag. Coral Creek was a larger metropolis, but Badfish was finally beginning to hold its own after so many years of fighting and flailing against a downward spiral.

Leonard smiled; he felt proud, excited and a little bit nervous to walk through the main door of the business again. The ugly memories still loomed, but not like they once did. He knew time would help them to fade and eventually positive, healthy memories would take their place. He opened the door and stepped over the threshold to join his wife and friends in the refurbished lobby.

"Are we checked in already?" Leonard asked.

"Just about, Leonard," Phil answered. "Can you believe the difference?"

"Quite a change. Yeah, I can't believe it," he said, gazing around. "But the real credit goes to Donald Bickley. He's the one that plunked down thousands to make it all happen. I think that was the biggest shocker of it all."

"Hard to believe Bickley owns this too. You know, I heard a rumor that he's going to open up a new seafood place just over on Sandhill Avenue. I gotta hand it to him; he's really made some changes in Badfish."

"For the *better*, Phil. I'm so glad to see things changing for better these days. "

The men were interrupted by the young woman behind the service counter.

"Okay, I think we're all set. I have two rooms; one for the Mill party and the other right next door, for the Gentry party. You have king beds, a whirlpool tub and a large flat screen television in each room. Our porter, Ed, will see that you get settled. Is there anything else I can help you with at this time?"

"This is perfect, Tracy. It's great to see you again. How do you like being manager of the new Inn?"

"It's truly a miracle for me. It's so much better than where I worked before...with Karl. I never dreamed how much things would change. Well, that they even *could* change. When Mr. Bickley came to me with the idea of being manager here, I didn't know what to say. I think I even told him that I might leave the area. But he was pretty convincing and told me how much he wanted to turn Badfish around. After that, I couldn't help but get on board."

"I'm really happy for you, Tracy. I'm so glad things worked out. And now, I think my party is ready to relax and then partake in some late afternoon shopping. Right, my dear?"

"Shopping first, Leonard, then you can relax all you want," his wife chided.

Both couples laughed. They waved to Tracy, grabbed their suitcases and followed Ed to their rooms.